Paige wondered what Caleb was thinking.

"After tonight," he said, "after actually seeing this place…do you still want to be involved with the center?" He spoke so quietly, she had to lean even closer.

Did she? Paige bit her lip. "Yes. Of course." If only to prove she could.

"But I don't understand," he said. "You've now—"

"You don't just back down from something you've thought about for years." Paige tried to keep the quiver out of her voice.

"It's not safe, Paige. Don't you see that?" He braced one hand on her car and one hand on his truck. "For instance, tonight—what if I hadn't stayed and made sure you got to your car safely? This is a dangerous city."

"So you keep saying."

He shoved his hands into his pockets. "I'll continue to remind you of that until you get it."

Paige folded her arms, hiding her hands so he wouldn't see that they were shaking.

Why couldn't he understand?

Books by Jessica Keller

Love Inspired

Home for Good
The Widower's Second Chance

JESSICA KELLER

A Starbucks drinker, avid reader and chocolate aficionado, Jessica writes both romance and young adult fiction. As a child, Jessica possessed the dangerous combination of too much energy coupled with an overactive imagination. This pairing led to more than seven broken bones, countless scars and even more story ideas. Jessica holds degrees in both communications and biblical studies. She lives in the Chicagoland suburbs with her amazing husband, beautiful daughter and two annoyingly outgoing cats. Jessica loves interacting with readers. Find all of her contact information at www.jessicakellerbooks.com.

The Widower's Second Chance

Jessica Keller

HARLEQUIN® LOVE INSPIRED®

Recycling programs
for this product may
not exist in your area.

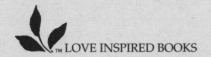 ™ LOVE INSPIRED BOOKS

ISBN-13: 978-0-373-87905-2

THE WIDOWER'S SECOND CHANCE

www.Harlequin.com

Printed in U.S.A.

He who was seated on the throne said,
I am making everything new.
Then he said, Write this down, for these words are
trustworthy and true.
—*Revelation* 21:5

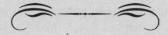

First and foremost, thank you and love to my husband and beautiful daughter, who overflow my heart with love, making it possible for me to have the energy and encouragement to keep writing. Also to the members of the BCGE who helped me brainstorm and add layers to both Caleb and Paige, the story wouldn't have been written without you all. Many thanks to my parents, who are always happy and willing to watch my baby so I could write—you both believe in me, and that has made all the difference in my journey. Lastly to the lovely Lisa Marie, who has asked me for years when I'd start writing *"those stories about the tourist town in Michigan"* that I told her about back in our college days. For you, Lisa, Goose Harbor now lives.

Chapter One

That sure smelled like fire.

Caleb Beck backed out from his crouched position under the sink and laid down the wrench. Hopefully the patch on the pipe would work. "Mags! Are you cooking something?"

He clomped over to the industrial oven he'd installed at the bed-and-breakfast a few years ago. Cool to the touch. He peeked inside, just in case. Empty.

The inn had seven guest bedrooms, and four of the rooms had their own fireplaces. He sniffed the air and turned in a circle, his fingers looped on his tool belt. The smell didn't come from upstairs. Out the window over the kitchen sink, Caleb spotted the inn's owner, Maggie West, working in the garden. It would be just like his absentminded sister-in-law to not follow city code and burn something out in the yard.

He yanked open the back door. "Maggie. Are you burning something? Leaves, maybe?"

Maggie rolled her eyes at him, her hands on her hips and her curly brown hair puffing out in every angle imaginable. "Burning leaves at the end of summer? We have months yet for that. Don't tell me you hit your head in there."

Caleb growled. Should have known he wouldn't get a straight answer out of her. Maggie had been stubborn since they were kids playing on the beaches of Lake Michigan together.

He let out a long breath. *Be patient.* "Well, something is burning, and if you're just going to stand there…"

"It's probably faulty work done by my handyman." A laugh in her voice, she bent back down to tend to her garden.

"But I'm your handyman."

"Like I said."

He shoved through the back door and his eyes landed on the door that led to the basement. *Of course.* These old Victorians came complete with ancient and terrible wiring. Sure, the homes filled the tourist town of Goose Harbor with charm, but the laws against changing historical landmarks made it difficult to improve the buildings when safety came into play. Maggie might not take him seriously, but the whole place could go up in a heap of smoke if he didn't act fast. Caleb hurtled down the stairs, taking them two at a time.

The sight that met him made him freeze for a moment.

A woman he'd never seen before hunched over a metal tub in the middle of the cold floor. Her blond hair splayed across her face and blocked him from seeing her expression. Pieces of paper fanned out in all directions around her.

He took a step forward. She didn't look up. Caleb scooped up one of the papers. A letter.

Dear Paige…

Her shoulders trembled. "Never again."

Paige tossed a stack of folded papers onto the small fire

burning in the tub. Flames licked the edge of the bin as the paper started to curl and turn black. Next, she grabbed a mound of white fabric from beside her. If she tossed that wispy bunch of cloth into the small tub, the fire would get out of control. Not to mention smell awful.

He crossed to where she sat on the ground.

Almost in a daze, Paige lifted her arms, ready to stuff the white pile of fabric into the fire.

Caleb caught her wrists. "What are you, crazy? Don't do that." He tugged what now registered in his head as a dress out of her clutches.

Paige slammed her hands onto her hips. "Give that back."

Caleb tossed it out of her reach. She moved to go after the dress, but he grabbed her slender shoulders, and she finally looked at him. When her crystal-blue eyes locked on his, something warm curled inside his chest. He knew enough about women to know only one thing could cause those huge raccoon marks on her face. She'd been crying. Not just crying—sobbing. But even the running mascara couldn't mask her simple beauty. The splash of freckles across her cheeks, delicate nose and pursed lips as she exhaled…everything about her screamed *protect me*.

Had he ever been able to deny someone who needed help?

Caleb shook that thought away. He'd had the opportunity to protect more than one person he cared about and failed. Miserably. Never again.

He didn't deserve another chance.

A thin breath rattled out of her, and she shrank away from him. "I'm sorry. I don't know what I'm…I'm…" Paige looked like a scared animal begging a hunter not to shoot her.

"What were you doing?" Caleb kept his voice low and even.

"Can you please hand me my wedding dress?"

"Your...?" His eyes darted to the white pool of fabric he'd thrown to the corner of the basement. The girl was going to shove a wedding dress into the fire? What could have happened to her? "You can't burn that in here. It's not safe. Besides, a wedding dress is something to keep forever."

"Forever. Ha. Forever doesn't exist." Paige ran the back of her hand under her eyes and pushed up to her feet. Brushing past him, she scooped up the dress. "I can do whatever I want with it."

Caleb tugged the dress away from her. "Not toss it in that fire. In fact—" He strode past her to the sink near the washer and dryer and filled a pitcher with water. Walking back to the small metal tub, he doused the fire inside. The flames hissed as they died.

"You had no right." She crossed her arms over her chest and her foot tapped on the cement floor. Too bad the petite woman couldn't have looked menacing if she tried.

"And you have no right trying to burn down Maggie's inn."

"I wasn't going to—I promise I won't put it in the fire." She yanked a hair tie off her wrist and pulled her hair into a quick, messy bun. "It's been a bad day."

He took a step closer. Yes, this woman was beautiful. Of that there was no doubt. Despite her obvious grief and the spotty lighting in the basement, Paige's features were stunning—legs a mile long and honey-colored hair a man couldn't help but want to run his hands through. Her blue eyes were deep with locked secrets, kind of like an animal in a cage at the shelter—a little sad yet with the promise of hope. A dusting of freckles formed striking constellations on her cheeks. They were cute, making her seem approachable even in her present state of distress.

What was she doing here? "Who are you, anyway?"

She lifted her chin. "I live here."

"Listen. I know everyone in this town and I have never seen you in my life. Who are you?"

Her lips quivered. "Can I just have the dress back? Please?"

"Not if you're going to try to do something crazy with it again." He moved his hands behind his back so she couldn't make a grab at the fabric.

She balled her fists up at her sides. "I'm so tired of people telling me what I can and can't do." She marched toward him, bringing along a sweet, flowery smell that made him want to lean closer even with the blaze in her eyes.

Her pointer finger jabbed into his chest. "You can't tell me what to do."

"I don't know what you're talking about, but—"

"It's just… I can't believe—" She dissolved into a mess of tears and ragged breaths. Hands covering her face as her shoulders hunched, her knees began to buckle.

Caleb dropped the dress and caught her elbows before she hit the ground. She wasn't even trying to stand anymore. He had to press her to his chest and wrap his arms around her just to keep her upright. Her head fit right into the place next to his heart. "Shh. Hey. You're okay."

Okay? Should he have said that? It's not like he knew her problems. But no man in the world could handle a woman when she cried like that. He didn't even know her and her tears were making his heart bunch into a knot.

He tightened his hold a bit. "Did someone harm you? Are you in any sort of danger?"

One of her fists pounded against his shoulder three times before her fingers worked open and bunched the fab-

ric of his flannel shirtfront. "How could he? I was ready....
Life was set.... How could he?" She sniveled into his shirt
right next to his heart.

"I'm sorry. Whatever happened, I'm sorry you had to
go through it." He rubbed a circle on her back.

Paige rested her forehead against his chest and took a
few rattling breaths. He fought the foolish urge to bury
his nose in her soft hair. Not counting his sister or Maggie, how long had it been since he held a woman in his
arms? Two years.

The washing machine along the south wall clicked and
started whirling. The tiny legs of the machine clattered
against the cement with a high-pitched scratching sound.
Maggie probably overfilled the thing, again.

The sound snapped the woman in his embrace back to
attention.

Paige pushed out of his arms. "Oh. I'm so sorry. How
stupid of me. You must think that I..."

He held up a hand. "You don't have to explain." He
handed her the wedding dress.

"Thank you," she mumbled.

Caleb glanced up at the ceiling as if he could find directions on how to deal with distraught women written up
there. A stuffed snowman grinned back at him. Nothing
but beams packed with Maggie's decorations for all the
different holidays.

He wouldn't leave the woman alone in the basement in
case she did something else irrational, but he could hold
his tongue and give her a minute to collect herself. Besides,
it's not like he could help her if she asked. He'd never been
able to help anyone before.

Not really.

Stop acting crazy.
Paige Windom took a long, deep breath. What a way to

start life in a new town. Good thing Dad couldn't see her now. *Windows don't crack.* At least, that was what he always said. Then again, he'd lost his right to speak into her life. Cheaters and liars don't get to give advice.

Why wouldn't this man leave her alone? Her pity party was supposed to be an invitation-only thing. Table for one.

She didn't need a stranger seeing her in this state because this wasn't her. She organized everything, made to-do lists and had every lesson plan she'd ever written in a color-coded binder. Not that she'd admit it to anyone, but she even kept an Excel spreadsheet of her wardrobe to help match outfits for work. But well-laid plans hadn't led to dreams coming true. Not once. So maybe being rational wasn't worth it.

She sank to her knees.

Her fingers traced over the beadwork on the dress in her hands. The perfect Pronovias gown—an A-line organza with a sweetheart neckline, complete with a cascade of ruffles. It had taken thirteen shopping trips to find the perfect dress. Thirteen. She should have known better.

She hadn't cried when she discovered Bryan with another woman and hadn't even shed a tear on the three-hour drive from Chicago to Goose Harbor. But for some reason, as she unpacked her bag in the little room on the back side of the inn, her body started to ache. It felt like a bad case of heartburn, but more painful. And no matter how tightly she pressed a pillow to herself, the hurt in the pit of her stomach remained.

Would she have to walk through the rest of life feeling numb?

Sure, she wanted independence, but no one told her how abandoned being free felt.

Floorboards above her creaked, and the sound drew her back to the present. A damp, mildew smell clung to the cracked cement along the walls of the basement. The other side of the room still boasted a dirt floor. Sunlight filtered in through the basement's window wells.

The man in the basement with her worked his bearded jaw back and forth. Had she really just tossed herself into his arms? Quite the first impression. Paige felt her cheeks begin to burn. What must he think of her?

He hooked his hands on his tool belt. The man's silhouette against the evening sunlight outlined broad shoulders as his flannel shirt molded over coiled biceps. When he held her, he'd smelled like a midnight rainstorm, fresh with a slight scent of pine trees. His athletic form made him look ready to build a house from scratch or chop down a tree. The man was all strength, but carried a gentle reassurance about his person all the same.

Regardless of his relaxed pose, he would be able to move quickly if she did something reckless with her dress again. Not that she planned to.

The man took a slow step closer and then knelt down in front of her. "Miss, are you all right?" His forehead creased. Only a foot or two away, she locked her gaze with his for the first time. His eyes were warm—the color of hot chocolate laced with cream.

Paige swallowed hard. "I'm okay."

He raised a brow. "Are you sure? You could talk to me, if that would make things better. I'll listen." His voice was a balm. Strong and reassuring.

Stop. Stop analyzing him. She hadn't come to Goose Harbor to check out the first man she bumped into. Not the first or the fifteenth.

"This isn't how I usually am. You caught me at a bad time." Paige rose from the floor, the dress clutched to her stomach. Maybe she'd sell the thing at a consignment shop in town. At least get some money out of it to help save toward a home of her own. Then strange men couldn't wander downstairs and find her during an off moment, and she wouldn't be able to embarrass herself again.

Although, the sooner she found a place of her own, the more the loneliness might seep in.

She set the dress on top of the washing machine. No need to bring it back to her bedroom. It would only serve as a reminder there.

The man got to his feet. "My name's Caleb. I'm friends with Maggie. Do you want me to go get her?"

Paige shook her head.

Caleb looped his hands on his tool belt again as if they needed to do something tangible. "Is there something I can do to help you? Anything?"

"Just go." Her voice cracked a little, even though she fought it.

"I'd feel better if I stayed here with you."

"I'm sure you have better things to do."

"Right now, making sure you're safe is the most important thing on my list."

Fine. She couldn't make Caleb leave—not if he shared a friendship with the inn owner, but she could make him feel unwelcome. Make sure she was safe? Unless he was the town greeter or an undercover cop, she didn't need him babysitting her.

Paige turned her back on him. A chill ran through her body. Why were basements so cold?

Caleb cleared his throat. "You're pretty quiet for a girl."

"For a girl, huh?" Paige fought back the first smile of the day as she turned to face him.

Like sunshine after a week of cloudy days, a full smile broke out across Caleb's lips, lighting up every plane and angle of his face. "I have a sister." His voice was bathed in tenderness. "She talks a mile a minute."

So he loved his family, had a nice voice and knew how to comfort a girl in need. Paige needed to get away from him. Quick. She couldn't afford to go soft on her vow against men so soon.

"I have to go. I'm sorry we had to meet like this." Paige rushed to the stairs and grabbed the railing. She looked back at Caleb. He opened his mouth as if he wanted to say something, but didn't.

Go, Paige. Just go. She'd gotten good at running away the past few months. At least, it was nice to think so. Without looking behind her again, she climbed the stairs and tried to forget the image of the concerned man in the basement with the gentle, chocolate eyes.

Caleb scrubbed his hand over the close-clipped hair on his chin. Women were confusing, plain and simple. At least the fire situation was under control. He grabbed the dress she'd left downstairs. Why had she made such a big deal of him giving it back to just leave it again?

"So, Smokey the Bear, what was it? Or like I suspected, was it all in your head?" Maggie's voice made him jump.

He turned to face her. "Do you have a new girl working here?"

She wiped the dirt from gardening on her ripped jeans. "I never did fill the cleaning position." Maggie leaned her hip against the basement wall. "But do you mean Paige? I'm letting her stay here for Principal Timmons until the tourists clear out and she can rent something more permanent in town. Let's see, she's about this tall. Pretty little blonde thing."

"Principal Timmons?"

"Yes. Paige is the new English teacher." Maggie smiled. The three English teachers' rooms were across the hall from where he taught science at the high school. So he'd be seeing a lot more of Paige.

"This is hers." He pressed the wedding dress into Maggie's hands. "But don't give it back to her if she's just going to try to light it on fire again."

"On fire?" Maggie's eyes grew big.

"Told you I smelled something."

Maggie hugged the dress to her chest. "That poor woman."

"That *poor woman* could have set your livelihood ablaze. Are you sure she's safe? You know, right in the head? I'd hate to see you in trouble." Caleb squeezed Maggie's shoulder.

"She's safe. I promise."

He searched her face. "You're the only sister-in-law I have." He offered a small smile.

Maggie brushed his hand away. "I keep telling you— you don't have to waste your life away worrying about little old me."

Right. She knew too well. The last time he worried about someone it had caused Maggie a lot of heartache, too.

Even though her words sliced, he shrugged. "Other than Shelby, who else do I have to worry about?"

"Caleb." She reached a hand toward him but let it drop to her side. "I didn't mean to—"

No more pity. He couldn't stand another person's concerned eyes on him. That was the problem with a small town—everyone knew what had happened to his wife and treated him differently because of it.

"Sink's fixed." He plodded up the steps. "See you later."

He didn't bother gathering his tools from Maggie's kitchen. She'd probably call him tomorrow with something else to patch at the inn. Not that he minded.

His sister, Shelby, might be waiting dinner on him at home. He checked his phone. No texts from her yet. He still had time.

Maybe he'd go shoot hoops at the school first.

Paige scoured mascara off her face so hard she left a red patch of skin.

What must Caleb think of her? Hopefully she'd never have to run into him again. If it came up in conversation she'd ask Maggie not to hire the same handyman next time or at least have Maggie warn her before she had him come for a job again. Facing him after she tossed herself into his arms would be nothing short of mortifying.

Okay. Let's face it. She probably would see him again. Hadn't he said he was friends with Maggie? More reason to find an apartment or home to rent somewhere else in town and soon as she could. That would be her first goal.

Paige let out a long breath of air.

Running away had never sounded like a good idea. But what else could she have done?

She sank onto the edge of the bed. This room was the size of Paige's closet at her parents' home, but in the same manner as the rest of the bed-and-breakfast, it was decorated like a charming English cottage. Good thing Principal Timmons had taken it upon himself to set up this living situation for her when he hired her last minute. And the owner, Maggie West, seemed nice enough. Although perhaps a little rough around the edges.

New starts were supposed to be exciting, right?

So why this heavy, hopeless feeling gnawing in the pit of her stomach?

Paige could hear Maggie in the kitchen, clanking spoons against bowls as she did prep work for tomorrow's breakfast. What to do? Paige didn't know anyone in the town of

Goose Harbor, but going to bed before the sun went down seemed a little too desperate.

No, she needed to do *something* to clear her mind. Without wasting another minute, she snagged her gym shoes out of the closet and tugged them on. Paige wouldn't go for a jog tonight, but she could scope out a trail to run for the next time she needed escape.

Maggie cleared her throat when Paige entered the kitchen.

"Are you okay, sweetie?" She wiped her hands on her green-checkered apron and gave Paige a sad smile.

"I'm guessing Caleb told you about my episode downstairs. I'm so sorry. That's not like me. I promise I won't act like that again."

"Don't even think about it. Believe me—men have done a number on my head one too many times to count. I guess that's why I'm resigned to spinsterhood." Maggie winked at her.

"Hardly. You're what, my age?"

"I think a couple years older. Thirty-four, but let's not go shouting that from the rooftops. You're going to be okay, you know that, right?" Maggie grasped Paige's hand, leaving some flour on her fingers.

"Sure. That's why I'm here. Time for something new." Paige tried to infuse life into her voice. She did like learning new things, and with her upbringing, she had so much to learn. But right now, it was the circumstances behind the uprooting of her life that dampened everything.

Maggie went back to punching a wad of dough on the counter. "I hung your dress up downstairs."

"Thanks." Paige touched her fingers to the couple of hair ties she always stored on her wrist. "Do you need help preparing anything? I don't know a lot about cooking, but I'm willing to learn."

"No need. I'm almost done for tonight. But I appreciate the offer." Maggie rubbed the back of her hand on her forehead, leaving more flour.

"Well, if you ever need me to, I do know one recipe for scones that I could make some time. It's about the only thing I know how to do in the kitchen." Paige laid her hand on the doorknob that led to the public section of the inn.

"I'll probably take you up on that at some point."

"Anytime. I'm going to go out for a little while." Paige walked through the door that led to the hotel portion of the bed-and-breakfast.

The common dining area boasted a large crystal chandelier that Maggie had told her was original to the mansion. The front parlor was rich with Persian carpets, flowered wallpaper, a grand piano and a stone fireplace surrounded by antique furniture. A towering grandfather clock ticked off the seconds as she passed by the grand, deep maroon carpeted staircase.

A bell tinkled as she pushed open the front door. She walked quickly down the sidewalk, passing her Mazda and the sign proclaiming: West Oaks Inn Bed-and-Breakfast.

Paige glanced over her shoulder at the Victorian mansion. Built in the Queen Anne style, sage clapboard gave way to pink-painted details and intricately carved wooden embellishments. Giant oak trees formed a line of soldiers up the driveway, protecting and shadowing the property. Cinderella might as well live there.

Too bad glass-slipper dreams only came true in storybooks.

Paige swung her arms, making herself walk faster.

Smaller homes on wide yards dotted the outskirts of the town. Even the most insignificant house here had more personality than any house found in the Chicago suburbs she had grown up in. Each one seemed to have a story—with a hundred years of history to be told.

Maybe this new start in Goose Harbor was all she needed. A fresh start. A new home.

No, not home. Nothing could ever feel like home again.

Leaving Illinois and all the dreams she'd clutched since childhood hadn't been easy. But staying meant seeing *him*—being reminded of *him*. Staying hadn't been a viable option.

At the bend in the road, the canopy of trees broke and the residential properties became closer together. Fresh Lake Michigan air mingled with the smell of someone barbecuing. Like giant sleeping bears, sand dunes hulked on both sides of the road. The anchoring trees grew through the shifting soil and hooded the road, only allowing slivers of sunlight to skip across her face when she turned onto Lake Front Drive.

A large town square made up the bustling portion of Goose Harbor. In the middle of the square was a large grassy area complete with a red band shell, a few park benches, a white gazebo and a small rose garden. A short distance from the square lay Ring Beach—named for the almost perfect half circle of soft sand that lined the shorefront. The calm, shallow waters at Ring Beach drew thousands of visitors to Goose Harbor every summer.

On the road, traffic slowed to a halt as a crop of buildings came into view. End-of-the-summer vacationers crowded the brick sidewalks that made up the downtown portion of Goose Harbor, clogging the roadways as they filtered between the homemade fudge shops, art galleries, unique mom-and-pop stores, ice-cream parlors and quaint restaurants built on stilts over the pier section of the waterfront. Women in high heels clip-clopped out of the way of darting children as old men sat watching the world go by from wooden benches lining the dock. White masts bobbed in the marina.

No wonder Goose Harbor had been voted one of the top five places to vacation in the Midwest.

Paige veered away from the cute downtown. Something told her to go to the beach, watch the waves roll in and pray. But there was no point. God didn't want to hear about her minuscule troubles. After all, He had wars and starving children to worry about. His time should be spent on situations that actually mattered to the world, not her. No, she didn't need to bother Him with her little issues.

Besides, when was the last time something she prayed for actually happened?

She followed the path that led to the high school. She stood in the parking lot, hands on her hips, and scanned the building. A group of people tossed a basketball around on the far outdoor court. A couple clad in neon spandex ran together around the track.

She could do this.

Sure, all her other teaching experience had been at inner-city schools in Chicago, but students in a tourist town couldn't be that different, not really. If she'd learned something while teaching it was that all teens needed one thing—someone to let them know that their life mattered and they had worth, as is.

Anyway, she'd relocated to Goose Harbor to volunteer at Sarah's Home—a nonprofit organization that helped at-risk youth. Over the past few years, Dad had donated to Sarah's Home because his college roommate, Mr. Timmons, was the head of the board. Dad might have used the place as a tax shelter, but Paige looked forward to the quarterly newsletter from Sarah's Home.

No one knew, but those newsletters had shaped her desire to work with inner-city students. She'd wanted to be a teacher since grade school, but only after poring over the updates and the Sarah's Home website had a passion sparked inside of her for at-risk youths.

After catching Bryan tangled up with a leggy redhead, Paige knew she needed to leave Chicago. All her friends were Bryan's friends. Her dreams near her childhood stomping ground were all too linked with the boy she'd known since junior high school.

No, leaving had been her only option.

Sarah's Home popped into her head immediately—her safe place. Now she could be a part of the nonprofit that had already shaped her life so much. In the midst of her trial, she could turn things around for the good and give back.

Yes, the chance to help at Sarah's Home had been the main draw to this area; finding a teaching job at the nearby high school had been a nice bonus. Her dad's friendship with Principal Timmons hadn't hurt, either. Timmons had been urging her to apply to his school ever since she graduated and was only too happy to call her when a last-minute position opened.

Who knew? Maybe in a few weeks she'd have a bunch of friends here…maybe that would be her in the middle of a neighborhood game of pickup.

Paige took a couple of steps forward, squinting to watch the basketball game. It looked like a bunch of teens, probably her future students. Maybe they were members of the high school's team getting in a practice before school started at the end of the week. A couple of elementary-school kids sat on the sidelines.

The tallest guy called for a break and walked over to where the children sat. The two boys hopped up when he offered them the basketball. The man motioned for them to follow him to the basket, where he took turns lifting both of them up to dunk the ball.

From a distance, she couldn't make out how old the man was, but his gesture warmed her heart and made her long for the family she dreamed of but wouldn't have. Perhaps those were the coach's sons. Either way, in her experience it was a rare trait in a man to choose to play with kids when he could be standing courtside joking with the older students.

When they called game again, Paige crept a bit closer. She took a seat on a wooden bench near the court.

The tallest man dribbled the ball, skirted past his opponent and sank the ball into the net with a *swoosh*. Caught up in the moment, Paige clapped.

The player turned around and locked gazes with her. Recognition hit her in the stomach like a punch.

Caleb.

She shot to her feet, spun around and picked her way across the field in the opposite direction.

So much for her hopes of never seeing him again.

Chapter Two

"Can we not talk about this right now?" Caleb dropped his voice and glanced around the Cherry Top Café to see if anyone was listening to him and Maggie. Burgers sizzled on the big grill in back and a grease tang hung thick in the air. A busboy clanked dirty dishes together as he cleared a nearby table. Tucked a block away from the popular town square, Cherry Top didn't rank high on the must-hit tourist list, but that's why Caleb ate there.

Maggie shoved the coleslaw around on her plate with her fork. "I'm not dropping this. Hear me out. It's like your life is on hold. You've mourned long enough. I hope you know that."

Mourned long enough? *Impossible.*

Caleb grabbed the saltshaker and slid it between both of his hands. "Seriously, Mags, leave it alone."

"I can't. You know, it's hard for me, too, but I can't keep digging in my heels hoping she'll come walking into the inn again, either. Because she's not going to."

"Do you honestly think you've moved on?"

Maggie pursed her lips and looked outside.

A fly skittered against the windowpane near Caleb's elbow, buzzing wildly in its attempt to break through the glass and get back out in the fresh air. Maggie grabbed the menu and banged the heavy papers against the window, ending the fly's struggle for good.

She exhaled a long breath. "Besides, you're the only family around that I have left to bug, so you have to indulge my meddling whims."

"Not on this." He shoved his plate toward the center of the table and tossed his napkin on top.

Maggie reached across the table and laid her hand over his. "You're still young and have so much of your life left. My sister would have wanted you happy. You know that, don't you?"

He snaked his hand from hers and dropped it in his lap under the table. "I am happy." *Sometimes.* Like during the school year with students filing into his science classroom, or at the church's summer camp when the teens talked at the end of the session around the fire pit about how much they had learned and grown that week.

Maggie offered a sad smile. "Well, Caleb Beck, you could have fooled me."

Caleb leaned forward and lowered his voice. "If you wanted to talk about this we could have done it at the inn instead of out in public."

People stared at him enough. *Poor Caleb.* He didn't need to add this conversation to the list of reasons to pity him. Gossip had a tendency to spread like lice in Goose Harbor, especially among the year-round residents. He didn't need anyone overhearing Maggie and thinking he couldn't hack it as a teacher or youth-group volunteer, or continue on at Sarah's Home. He was so tired of being treated like he was broken.

The high school's soccer coach, a heavyset man in his mid-forties, walked past their table and waved his spoon at Caleb. What was the man's name? Caleb offered a po-lite smile back.

Maggie tugged the giant clip out of the back of her hair, rearranged it a little and pinned up her hair again. Only, she missed a chunk of unruly curls, making it look like a crazy peacock feather coming out of the side of her head. "It's not like I planned to dive into all this, but I felt like I needed to tell you that I'm okay with you dating again. In case you were worried about that. If you find the chance to have love again, you should. Okay? That's all I'm going to say about it. Promise."

He kept his eyes trained out the window at the tourists strolling toward the dock. "Thank you."

The waiter dropped off their check, and Caleb had the man stay while he pulled out the correct change and enough for a tip. "Just keep everything."

Maggie crossed her arms and leaned back in her seat. "You don't have to pay for me all the time."

"Besides my sister, who else am I spending my money on these days?" Caleb leaned a little to put his wallet into his back pocket.

"How's your sister doing?"

Scared. Lonely. Worried. He shrugged. "Shelby's the same as always, I guess."

"Okay, I know I said I wouldn't bring it up again, and after this I won't." Maggie splayed her hands onto the table. "But there's this girl in my Bible-study group at church. She's cute and she really loves the Lord. I think you two would—"

"Leave it alone, Mags. Just let it be." Caleb worked his jaw back and forth.

The image of the lake outside the window suddenly blurred. "I'm not going to date her." He blinked a couple of times. "I have no intention of dating again. Ever. Got it?" He snatched his baseball hat off the table and jammed it onto his head. "I need to get home. I have to be at work early tomorrow."

Maggie gave a small nod and clutched her purse as she scooted out from the bench seat. Caleb handed over her coat without a word. On his way past the front desk he took a handful of waxy mints from the large bowl by the register and tossed them all into his mouth. They tasted like medicine-flavored chalk—a fitting end to the day.

He held open the door for Maggie. "I'll stop by on Saturday to fix the drainpipe."

She nodded and clicked the button to make her car chirp. Good thing she knew better than to offer him a ride home. A man needed space for his mind away from everyone crawling over every inch of his hometown.

At least he did.

Caleb shoved his hands in his pockets and took the long route. Frogs croaked in the nearby stream, signaling the end of another summer evening. Near the residential section of the lakefront, a fishy smell hung in the air—which meant a fish fry at Cherry Top next Friday.

A car full of teens flashed their headlights at him and pulled alongside the gravel on the road. They blasted the horn, all waving, as the car came to a stop.

"Mr. Beck!" One of the girls hung out the back window. "I have you for second period."

He smiled and waved. "Only three more days until classes start. What are you guys up to tonight?"

Please don't say a party. The town had seen a recent uptick in teen mischief down at the beaches at night. Lots of empty beer bottles and spent fire pits most mornings made Caleb worried for their safety. If only the town provided other outlets for the students during the summer.

Most of their parents were too busy running shops in town to keep a good eye on their kids.

"Oh, you know. Same old." The girl rolled her eyes. "Is it true we dissect cats in your class? Because if so, I might have to transfer out." She pulled a face like she was gagging.

Caleb shook his head. "We stopped using cats years ago. It's all on a computer now."

"Good, because that's sick. Not to mention, ethically wrong." She smacked the boy in the car next to her in the shoulder. "You liar!"

"You guys be smart tonight." Caleb made his way back to the sidewalk.

"Of course, Mr. Beck!" A couple of the teens laughed. The car peeled away and sped down the street.

Another car full of teenagers honked and waved at him as he walked home. He kept his hands in his pockets and gave them a nod. Hopefully he could at least plaster on a smile for them when classes started later in the week.

Paige glanced at the missed calls on her phone—three from Mom, but no voice mail. Mom probably wanted to see how she liked Goose Harbor, right? That, or she had news about the house. Right before Paige left home, her parents informed her they were planning to downsize and travel more. Not that she'd tell them, but Paige hoped her childhood home didn't sell quickly. It would be nice to have somewhere familiar to return to if the situation in Goose Harbor didn't work out after the first year.

She pictured her mother, already put together for the day and decked out in her usual pearls and heels.

The phone vibrated again.

"Morning, Mom, you're up early. You caught me trying to get ready for my first day of work." Paige looked between the two outfits she'd laid out on her bed.

"I wish you would reconsider leaving Chicago."

Paige closed her eyes and pinched the bridge of her nose. "Not this again. Please. I don't want to have this conversation right now."

"You were so happy here. The plan had always been for you to stay close by. I can't imagine you living somewhere else."

"Plans change, Mom." Paige yanked a hair tie from her wrist and worked it around in her hand.

"They don't have to."

Paige sank into the wicker chair beside her bed. "They did. You'll see. This is for the better. Anyway, I like it here."

Mom sighed. "I always took you for more of a fighter, Paige. Someone who would stand her ground. Stay and tackle things."

"You know, sometimes leaving is fighting. Standing up for myself meant getting away, don't you see that? It would have been easier to stay there, living with you and Dad, letting you guys take care of everything for me, and carrying on with my life. Leaving was harder, Mom. Much harder." She started to pull her hair into a bun and froze. Leave it down. She wanted to wear it down for work today.

"If you ask me, I think you're making too big of a deal about everything."

"Too big of a deal?" Paige hated the tremble in her voice.

"Calling off a wedding that cost your father and me so much money without trying to fix your problems with Bryan, first? That's overreacting at its best."

Except that she'd been able to get most of the money back. All but the security fees.

"I don't think sleeping with some woman a month before his wedding is a problem that we could have just fixed." Just saying the words made the back of Paige's eyes throb again. *Don't cry.* No more tears because of Bryan. He didn't deserve them.

Mom sighed. "I don't know what to tell you, honey. From time to time, men make mistakes—"

Don't say it.

"Like Dad?" The back of Paige's eyes burned the second the words left her mouth. She shouldn't have said that. She had promised her mom she wouldn't bring it up again. "I'm sorry." Paige waited. "Are you still here?"

"I'm not trying to butt into your life." Mom's voice took on a flat tone. "But you need to think through all your options with a *rational mind.* All those childhood books and movies, well, they lied, sweetheart. There is no *one* true love. There is no perfect match. There are just people, and you make it work because you made a promise to." Her mother's voice took on a stern, almost scolding tone.

Paige's stomach churned.

"Even with his unfortunate mistake, Bryan is still a good catch. That boy is going to be something big someday, and I don't want you to regret anything down the road. Believe me, I know all the feelings you have right now and how difficult it is." She stopped, but started again when Paige didn't jump in to fill the silence. "What sort of men are you bound to meet in who-knows-where Michigan? I'm sure there won't be a senator's son chasing you there."

"Maybe I'm not looking for a man." Prepared for a verbal assault, Paige gripped the armrest of the wicker chair.

"At your age, you should."

Paige rested her forehead in her free hand. "I'm sorry about all the money you guys lost."

"I know, honey. It's just a shame what a waste it all turned out to be. Bryan really is a nice boy."

She needed to change the subject. Talking about anything else was better than this. "So have you guys decided if you're going to put the house on the market?"

"The for-sale sign is already in the yard."

"So fast?"

"Yes. The first open house is this weekend."

After hanging up, Paige shoved the conversation to the back of her mind. Bryan couldn't ruin today. *From time to time, men make mistakes.*

Mistakes and choices were two very different things.

She pulled on jeans and a loose knit shirt. From the paperwork she'd received it looked like they'd be in and out of training for most of the day, but maybe she'd be able to stay late and start putting together her classroom. If so, that would be dusty work that included a lot of time organizing books on the floor. Jeans wouldn't impress her coworkers, but they were the best option.

She'd walk to work as long as the weather stayed nice. Doing so didn't leave her a lot of time for breakfast this morning, but it would help her save money to put into her dream-house account. Living with Maggie so far seemed fun, but Paige needed to prove to herself that she could make it without depending on anyone else.

The mouthwatering smell of baked cinnamon and frying bacon propelled her out of her bedroom. Grabbing her bag, Paige rushed out to the kitchen.

Flour and eggshells covered the large island in the center of the kitchen, and Maggie whirled around, grabbing muffins and restarting the coffee machine. She wore her curly hair clipped back.

An elderly woman teetered by the sink, loading dishes into the washer. Her nylons wrinkled around her ankles like elephant skin, and her flowered dress would make a queen bee envious. A silver waterfall of hair dived down her back.

Maggie noticed Paige and smiled. "Sorry about the mess. Breakfast is the busiest time around here. Every room is booked today with people trying to take in the last of the summer."

"Right." Paige laughed. "I forgot the whole breakfast part of a bed-and-breakfast."

"I'll see you after school." Maggie backed through the set of doors that led to the hotel portion of the inn.

The old woman dried her shaky hands off on a kitchen towel. "You must be the pretty new schoolteacher that Magpie told me about. You're going to be the one teaching Shakespeare and those sorts of books, right?"

"Yes, I'm Paige." She extended her hand.

"Ida Ashby. I live right next door, and you're welcome to pop by any old time."

"Thanks. I better head out to the school. I don't want to be late on my first day." With the kitchen looking like a Tasmanian devil had spun through it on a tirade, skipping breakfast sounded like the best option.

"Wait one moment, dear, and I'll walk halfway there with you."

"Mrs. Ashby, there's no need to—"

"And it's just plain Ida, if you don't mind." Ida pulled her coat down from a peg by the back door, scooped up a bundle of flowers from the counter and motioned for Paige to leave with her.

Paige took a deep breath and followed after. The sound of Lake Michigan lapping against the shore worked the tightness from her muscles. She batted away the earlier conversation with her mother. Today she'd focus on new beginnings.

Ida looped her arm through Paige's. The skin on her hands was thin and delicate like the finest tissue paper. "I like to come help Maggie sometimes in the morning when I'm feeling up to it. The poor dear is always taking on too much alone. I'm glad she has you for companionship, at least for a little spell."

"Have you lived next door a long time?" Paige matched her longer strides with Ida's shorter, slower pace.

Good thing she'd skipped eating at the inn. If Ida changed her mind and decided on walking the whole way to school, Paige might end up very late.

"Oh. Long enough. I came to Goose Harbor with my husband many years ago." Ida unwound her arm from Paige's and stopped as they approached a small bridge.

A metal railing bordered the sidewalk to protect people from falling off into the stream below. Water churned over rocks and surged down a path that led to a mill. The wheel of the mill slapped the water in a steady rhythm. Below the mill, the water pooled, creating a large pond where ducks squawked at each other and sunned themselves on the muddy shore.

Ida shuffled to the edge of the metal fencing. "Here's the place. It's kind of you to be company for me on my errand today."

Errand?

Paige hooked her hand on the strap of her messenger bag and took a step backward. "Actually, I need to make sure I get to the school on time."

"It'll only take a moment." Ida tugged a dead bouquet from the railing and handed it to Paige.

The dried buds crinkled in her hands. Paige peeked at her watch. Fifteen minutes until she needed to check in at the gymnasium.

Ida worked the fresh bouquet into the place where the

decaying one had been. Her fingers shook, making her miss the metal rings a couple of times. "I leave new flowers here every week for my Henry." Ida pressed her palms to her lips and kissed them. Then she fanned out her hands in a gesture that sent the kiss down the river. "He fell right here. We were on a morning walk and his heart failed him exactly where you're standing." Her voice grew softer with each word.

Paige cupped Ida's hands. "I'm so sorry for your loss."

"Oh, it's been years now." Ida let out a long breath. "But I still miss Henry every single day. That's how it is with true love, you know? It doesn't go away just because the person does. Your heart just keeps right on waiting for them."

If true love existed, maybe Ida was the only one to have found it. Because Paige sure hadn't. And neither had her mother. Men like Henry no longer existed.

"I'm sure Henry was an amazing man." Paige offered a reassuring squeeze.

"He served as mayor to this town for thirty-six years. A very good man. I know some people think I'm silly for leaving flowers here every week. Thank you for being kind to a crazy old lady." Ida's eyes filled with tears.

"No, thank *you* for letting me come along." Paige bit her lip. She'd be late to work, but seeing Ida like this tore at the raw place in her heart where Paige stored her own hurt and pain. What would it be like to love someone like Ida loved her Henry? "Are you going to be all right? I feel bad leaving you here like this."

Ida pulled a handkerchief from her purse and dabbed at her eyes. "Don't worry about me. People see tears and get all flustered and want them to stop. But know what I say? It's okay to mourn the life you thought you were going to have. You can't heal if you don't allow yourself that much."

"As long as you're sure you're okay."

Ida smiled, revealing a smudge of red lipstick on her front tooth. "Now, you better skedaddle on down to the school, and I'll go on back and help Maggie clean up. If I made you late, just tell them you were humoring Ida and everyone will understand."

Paige jogged into the parking lot with two minutes to spare. She joined the line of teachers near the end of the gymnasium.

A woman with spiked black hair, who looked about her age turned around and offered a smile. "I'm Bree. You must be the new English teacher."

Maybe she looked as out of place as she felt.

Paige clutched the strap on her bag. "Am I the only new person this year?"

"Yes, and it's been the talk among the teachers for the past week."

They arrived at the temporary desk set up near the front of the large room. Portable tables and chairs arranged in four rows occupied most of the space in the gym. Paige and Bree each gathered a training manual and a teacher binder.

"Want to sit with me?" Bree snagged a table two rows back, near the edge.

"Definitely. I don't like feeling like the only one here no one knows."

"You'll be fine." Bree opened her binder. "I hope you slept well because these teacher-institute days are boring, but you probably know that from your last position."

The principal strolled up to the microphone near the front of the gym. "This is your warning. We'll start reviewing safety protocol in five minutes, so if you want to grab a bagel or coffee, I'd do so now." In jeans and a hooded sweatshirt bearing the school's name and a roaring panther on his chest, the man didn't look his age.

Paige leaned closer to Bree. "In Chicago, I sat through a training with five times as many teachers crammed into a smaller room with no air-conditioning."

Bree scrunched her forehead. "Well, that explains it. We knew whoever got hired must have amazing experience." She jutted her thumb to indicate a woman seated in the back row. "Steer clear of Amy Lambert, okay? She works as a part-time aide and applied for your position. To say she was angry about getting passed over for the job would be an understatement."

Paige peeked over her shoulder at Amy. The woman's head was bent down as she read something on the table in front of her. Her brown roots showed along the part of her bleached blond hair. She wore a deep purple suit, which made her the best dressed person in the room.

A couple of teachers shuffled by with plates full of fruit and Danishes.

Paige pressed her hand over her stomach when it grumbled. "I think I'm going to go grab a bagel. Do you want anything?"

Bree yawned. "A cup of coffee would be great."

When Paige made it to the back of the room she found a couple of onion bagels and a pile of energy bars. The bars looked like freebies that had spent the better part of a year stuffed in the back of someone's filing cabinet. An onion bagel would have to do. Next, she made her way to the coffee machine.

"If everyone could please take your seats I would like to begin." Principal Timmons's voice boomed over the loudspeaker.

Paige snatched her plate and Bree's cup of coffee and whirled around to rush back to her table.

Instead she smacked into the man standing behind her. *Caleb.* Of course.

Coffee splattered across his shirt and ran down her arms. Caleb yelped and all the papers he'd been holding fluttered to the ground.

The foam cup hit the floor with a loud, hollow *thunk*.

Was everyone staring at them? Klutz. That would be the first impression she made to all her coworkers.

Paige rapid-fire blinked. "I didn't know you worked here."

"So you pour coffee on me?" Caleb laughed.

"I'm sorry. I'm so sorry." Paige grabbed a wad of napkins and dabbed at his soaked oxford shirt.

Caleb caught her hand and held it. "Hey, I'm kidding. The coffee's not even hot."

"Still. Your shirt is ruined. Coffee doesn't come out easy."

"It's fine." His hand over hers was warm in a comforting way. She finally met his inviting chocolate gaze and he winked at her. A girl could get used to those eyes… lost even.

Except, Paige had promised herself she wouldn't let another man into her life.

Breaking eye contact, Paige tugged her hand away from his and took a step backward.

She needed to be careful around Caleb. Much more careful.

Chapter Three

"Careful." Caleb reached for Paige as she skittered backward into the table.

Her blundering caused a landslide of power bars to fall in a crescendo of crinkling plastic onto the gym floor. Her bagel bounced off the toe of his boot. He grabbed her arm before she toppled over, as well.

Coffee dripped down his side, and the front of his button-down was wet enough to wring out. Good thing the pot of coffee had been sitting out for so long that the liquid wasn't hot enough to burn him. Or Paige for that matter.

"I'm such a klutz." The woman turned toward him again. Paige froze when her crystal-blue eyes locked with his. She frowned, drawing his gaze to her lips. They had something shimmery on them that made them inviting.

He shook that thought away.

"We'll have to stop running into each other like this." He let go of her wrist.

She glanced over her shoulder and he followed her gaze. The entire room had gone quiet. All the teachers turned in their seats and stared at them. Some of them smirked and whispered to each other. There were gossips in the crowd and people who liked to cause trouble for fun. Most of them had grown up in Goose Harbor. While tourists were welcome with open arms in the shopping district, the locals weren't always as cordial with newcomers when it came to the other aspects of town.

Something inside told him to step in front of the new teacher and block her from their scrutiny. Shield her from pain like he'd done for his wife, Sarah, and sister, Shelby.

Although a lot of good that had done them.

Principal Timmons cleared his throat over the microphone. "Caleb, I see you've met our new English teacher, Miss Paige Windom. She'll be teaching freshman English and will also teach some of the senior level classes in our advanced-placement track." Timmons pulled a stool over the floor, the metal legs clanking. "Everyone—Paige comes to us from the big city of Chicago, and I'm confident she'll be an asset to our school."

The woman's cheeks turned a candy-apple red as the principal continued to talk.

Caleb reached around Paige and placed a fresh bagel on a paper plate and held it out to her.

"Peace offering?" he whispered.

"Shouldn't I be the one making amends?" She worked her bottom lip between her teeth. "Are you sure the coffee didn't hurt you?"

Caleb shook his head. "I was the one in your way." He leaned closer. "I didn't like this shirt anyway."

Paige tilted her head. "Really? I thought you looked nice." Then she eyed her shoes, as if they were suddenly the most fascinating things in the world. "I mean—dressed up."

A chuckle rumbled in his chest before he had a chance to rein it in. "You know, if we don't sit down they'll never stop staring."

"Right." She spun around, but then turned back and

touched his forearm before he could leave. "Would you be willing to do me a favor?"

Goose bumps raced up his arm. Probably just a reaction to the cold coffee on his skin.

"Sure." Caleb crossed his arms.

Principal Timmons tapped his mic. "Does this thing work?"

"Please." She studied her shoes again. "Don't tell anyone about the other day." Paige worked the bagel around and around in her hand.

"Of course not."

She gave a quick nod and scurried to her seat beside Bree. Caleb leaned against the back wall of the gym.

The principal ran through the safety protocol for inclement weather, but Caleb couldn't focus on anything Timmons said. Instead, he watched the back of Paige's blond head. What sort of secrets was she sharing with Bree? Nothing to do with a wedding dress—no, that secret was between him and Paige.

What had happened to her?

Not that it mattered.

Because he didn't care.

Not a bit.

Considering the talk with Mom and spilling coffee on Caleb, the day hadn't started out well, but the second half proved better than any dream Paige could have had. She sat on the floor of her classroom with classic novels fanned out in a circle around her. She ran her fingers over a book that held a collection of poems by Robert Frost as she tried to decide which one to read to start the first day of classes.

Air whispered through the leaves on the tree outside the windows. Her classroom faced east, which meant she didn't have a coveted view of Lake Michigan. On the plus side, the room would be splashed with sunlight for the better part of most days.

"Hi there." A voice in her doorway startled her. A man wearing too-short shorts and a whistle around his neck leaned against her doorjamb. Everything about him screamed *gym teacher*. "I'm Lenny. Didn't get to introduce myself after the session this morning. Sure wish I had."

"Nice to meet you." She smiled but kept her hands on the pile of books. Maybe he'd get the hint that she wanted to put together her room and not chat. She was basically finished for the day, but Lenny didn't need to know that.

Lenny sauntered into the room and propped his foot on the closest chair. "Timmons said you're from Chicago. Do you live close to the park with that big metal bean? You know, down by the lake in the Lap of Chicago."

"The Loop?"

"Yeah. You from there? The Loop?"

"No. Actually, I'm from the suburbs. It's easier to say Chicago though because everyone knows where that is. And that's where I taught, so a part of my heart does live there I guess."

He leaned his hands on his knee. "I have a picture of myself by that bean on my desk in my office. You should come see it. Afterward we could grab something to eat if you want."

Paige glanced down at her hands. "I…um…"

Bree's loud cough as she entered Paige's classroom saved her from answering. "Leave her alone, man. She just got into town."

Lenny glared at Bree as he left the room. He gave Paige one last smile. "If you still want to see that picture or go to dinner, you know where the gym is. I'll be testing out the weight room for the next hour or so."

Bree doubled over in laughter. "Promise me you won't fall for Lenny the Leech. Anyone but him, okay?"

"Is he always like that?" Paige fought a smile as she loaded books into her canvas bag to take home.

"Oh, sometimes he's much worse."

"I'll keep my radar up." She winked.

"Good, because there are a lot of cute, single guys in town. I wouldn't want you to judge all of Goose Harbor's bachelors based on Lenny."

"As far as I'm concerned, they can all be like him." Paige slung the canvas bag over her shoulder. The strap cut into her arm right away. Too many books, but she couldn't think of one she didn't want to bring home to help plan lessons. With her parents gone so often, books became the one, steadfast friend in her childhood.

"I promise they're not."

"It doesn't matter. Believe me, dating is the last thing on my list." Paige crossed to the windows she opened earlier to let in the late-summer breeze. She closed and locked each of them. "Actually, it's not even on my list."

"Is there someone back home?"

There *should* be. The familiar ache pushed its way into Paige's heart. "There's no one."

"Well, if you reconsider, I'll be your wingman…girl… you know what I'm saying."

"How about you tell me what's important about working here instead. You know, the unwritten rules." She walked into the hallway with Bree and closed her classroom door.

"Gotcha." Bree shoved a stick of gum into her mouth. "The parents here are really busy. Like—leave their home at five in the morning and get home at eight at night— busy. Most of them run shops in town and things like that to cater to the tourists so they expect us to keep their kids occupied. After-school activities are a big deal around here, especially now since there's been some rumors of mischief at the beaches in the evenings."

"Mischief?" Paige paused.

Bree stopped walking, too. "Spent bonfires. Empty beer bottles. The normal teenage stuff. Anyway, the PTA tends to turn on the teachers who aren't super involved if you know what I mean." She nodded to a couple of teachers who passed them as they made their way to the main entrance.

Paige stopped to reposition her bags. "What club are you in charge of?"

"Moi?" Bree laid her hand over her heart. "I run show choir." She sang the last part.

"Can't help you there. I know dogs that howl better than I sing." Paige shrugged.

"Well, try to think of something."

"I played volleyball all during college. I could probably coach."

Bree shook her head. "You won't believe it, but Amy's the head volleyball coach and I'm guessing you don't want to be her assistant."

Paige shrugged. "I don't even know her. For all I know she's nice and we could be friends."

"Keep dreaming. See you tomorrow." Bree waved, headed out to the bike rack and dumped her belongings into the basket attached to her eye-piercing yellow bike.

Paige balanced her teaching binder in one hand and her messenger bag and canvas sack full of books in the other. She'd work up a sweat on the trek home. At least she'd worn comfortable shoes. If she finished all her work early, she'd reward herself with a trip down to the beach. Her toes were itching to feel the sand.

Principal Timmons came running down the front steps after her, waving his arms like a bird learning to fly. "Miss Windom!" The principal wiped his forehead with the back of his sleeve. "I keep forgetting I'm not as young as I used to be."

"Mr. Timmons." Paige smiled at her father's old college roommate. The man had spent a couple of evenings every year around the Windoms' dinner table, but he was her boss now. She had to think of him that way. "I didn't get to thank you yet for hiring me."

"There's no need. You know I've wanted to offer you a position here ever since your dad told me you'd received your teaching degree. I'm just happy I had a job opening when you were ready to make the move." He wheezed out the words. "Now, if you have a second, would you mind coming back with me to my office? It'll only take a moment."

"Is something wrong?" Paige tensed.

"Not at all. I just need to go over something with you. Right this way."

Paige followed the principal down a hallway of dark blue lockers and through the door labeled Administration.

What could he want? Maybe there were still some papers to sign.

"Go ahead and take a seat in my office." Timmons held open the door.

She took a deep breath and turned the corner, but then stopped dead in her tracks. Caleb sat in one of the two chairs situated in front of the principal's desk. What was he doing there? Caleb had changed out of the shirt she'd spilled coffee on. Now he wore a deep maroon T-shirt that complemented his dark complexion, trim beard and mocha-colored hair. He looked more approachable, like that handyman from the other day.

His eyes narrowed a fraction in her direction.

Scratch approachable. He looked downright stern. Like

a man about to give a kid detention for daring to text during class.

A surge of ice ran through Paige's veins as a realization hit her. Had Caleb told Timmons about her breakdown yesterday? She had no other connection to him, save being a teacher. So why would they both be called to the principal's office? For all she knew Caleb could be in cahoots with Amy, the woman who wanted Paige's position. Really, why else would he be here? English and science were on different ends of the spectrum.... They didn't even teach the same grade. It had to be another reason.

Suppose he told Principal Timmons he saw her sobbing over her breakup, what would that mean? She couldn't lose her job for that sort of thing. Maybe get ordered to see the school counselor, but not lose her position. She couldn't. Not after upending her life to be here. After everything her father had done for him, how could Timmons listen to Caleb over her?

Her nails bit into her palms.

Why had she even trusted that he wouldn't tell? She knew better. If the past couple of years had taught her one thing it was that men lied. Dad. Bryan. Tommy. And Jay. All men.

It didn't matter.

She blinked back tears and ground her teeth together to keep from saying something she'd regret.

Principal Timmons dropped down into his swivel chair. "Go ahead and sit down, Paige. Caleb doesn't bite all that often." He chuckled over his own joke.

Paige set her bags on the ground and pressed her hands together. "I can explain."

Caleb scratched his chin. "I sure hope so, because I'd like to know what I did to get called to the principal's office so early in the year. Last year, when I helped with the senior prank, I understood, but—"

"Wait." She glanced back and forth between the two men, her gaze finally landing on Caleb. "You don't know why we're here?"

"No. Do you?"

"Then you didn't…?" *He didn't tell.* Her hands relaxed at her sides. The muscles in her shoulders eased. She crossed the room and took the chair beside Caleb.

Timmons rested his forearms on his desk. He looked from Caleb to Paige, then back to Caleb…then grinned and winked at Paige. "You both know that aside from my position at the school, I'm also the head of the board at Sarah's Home."

Paige nodded, but in her peripheral vision she caught Caleb brace his hands on the armrest of his chair and sit up a little straighter.

Principal Timmons continued, "So I'm speaking to you both from that capacity and not as your boss. In the past month—"

Caleb cleared his throat. "Sorry to interrupt, but if this is about Sarah's Home, why is Paige here?"

Timmons let out a long breath. "Because Paige is going to start working alongside you at Sarah's Home."

Her head jerked up. *Alongside?* As in, Caleb helped at the nonprofit, too?

"No." Caleb's knuckles went white. "No women from Goose Harbor. Not anymore. That's my rule. It's not negotiable. You know that."

His rule? Who was he to make a statement like that? Unless he was on the board, it didn't matter what he thought or said. Wait—was Caleb a board member?

She held her breath to keep from saying something she shouldn't.

First her father, then with Bryan—why did men think they could lay down some law that all the women in their lives had to follow? No one was going to control her again. No way. Not anymore. Forget watching her words.

Paige turned in her chair to face Caleb. "Well, great. I'm not from Goose Harbor so that works out just fine."

Caleb worked his jaw back and forth. "Same difference."

Timmons leaned forward in his chair. "Unfortunately, that's not the way Sarah set things up, and you of all people know that. The board holds power for all decisions. Especially when it comes to accepting volunteers."

"I get a say. Sarah's Home wouldn't exist if it wasn't for *my* wife." Caleb popped to his feet.

Wife? Paige tried to keep up with their conversation. Caleb was married? She glanced at his hand. No ring. But not all guys wore one.

Timmons lifted his hands and made a motion for Caleb to take his seat again. "Settle down, son. That's why I called you both in. I didn't want to spring anything on you. We need to talk about this."

"There's nothing to talk about." Caleb shook his head. His eyes fixed on Timmons. Clearly, Paige wasn't a part of the conversation any longer. "Can't you see how dangerous that would be? You were there at the meeting with the police chief. Crime against women like Paige has gone up in Brookside. Even more in the last two years. The gangs are looking for people like her. And I'm taking a guess that she's not certified in self-defense. It's not safe. End of discussion." He crossed the room and yanked the door open.

"Caleb," Timmons called after him.

But Caleb walked out the door. It slammed against the frame.

Paige ran the tips of her fingers back and forth over the

cheap, woven fabric on the armrest. Her heart pounded, clattering against her rib cage like a runaway train. She tried to control her breathing. Settle down.

Now what? She ran her fingers over the hair ties on her wrist.

Sarah's Home held a special place in her heart. A place no one—not even grumpy Caleb Beck—could take away.

Timmons sighed, bringing Paige back into the present conversation. "Don't worry. Caleb will come around."

"I hope so." Paige reached for her bags. "He…he can't keep me out, can he?"

"No. Like I said, the board holds the power."

She relaxed a bit. "What was it about Sarah's Home you wanted to see me about?"

"I was going to share that in the past month we've experienced an influx of teen girls coming to Sarah's Home. Caleb already knows that, but I planned to build a case so he would understand how important it is for you to join the team. This was all. I wanted Caleb and you to meet before you showed up at Sarah's Home. Offer him a chance to process. It just wouldn't have been fair to spring this on him in front of other people. You saw how he reacted. Unfortunately, we've let him have more control over decisions at Sarah's Home than we should have. After Sarah died, I guess the board didn't have the heart to say no to Caleb."

Paige looked down at the ground, studying the purple-specked carpeting. "So he was married to Sarah—the founder?" She'd read about Sarah's death in the newsletter a few years ago. But the section had been brief. No details. Just that the brave young woman had been killed while doing the thing she loved. A picture. A date for the funeral. No more information was ever released.

"Yes."

"And she died?"

Timmons frowned. "I'm afraid so. The whole town of Goose Harbor loved Sarah. A woman like her is impossible to replace."

Paige's stomach corkscrewed. "That's so sad."

Now Caleb's sudden gloom made sense. He seemed too young to be a widower. She'd never lost anyone close—well, not to death at least—so she couldn't identify with him, but her heart ached for him all the same. Behind his deep mocha eyes, Caleb hid pain—the loss of an irreplaceable woman. She'd remember that next time they talked.

"Very sad indeed, but the board still shouldn't have let him have his way in everything. I'm warning you from the beginning, he may have a very rough time with this transition. Having you at Sarah's Home will be hard on him. Don't hear me wrong. Caleb's a good man, and he does what he thinks is best—safest—for everyone." The principal straightened a pile on his desk. "Now here's a valid question. Are you afraid to be in Brookside after what he said?"

"No disrespect to Caleb, but I taught gang members in my classes in Chicago." Paige shrugged. "It's something you get used to. As weird as that sounds. We evacuated the school at least once a month for a bomb threat or something along those lines. It wasn't so fun when you had to rush out of the school in the middle of winter, but we managed."

"I figured as much. Between you and me, the place could use the infusion of some new blood. Now, there is one other thing I want to discuss with you if you have another moment." Timmons opened a manila file on his desk. "You played volleyball in college, right?"

"All four years." Paige tried to smile, but her mind was still on Sarah's Home. With Caleb against the idea, hopefully he wouldn't make her time there uncomfortable.

"Would you be willing to sit in on tryouts this year?

We had some troubles last year…accusations of unfair selections. I'd like the decision to be made by more than just the coach."

Who Bree had told her happened to be Amy. Great. But after what Bree said about teachers needing to be involved, she couldn't say no to her first chance. And it was only tryouts, not a commitment to coaching all season.

Paige chose her words carefully. "I guess I wouldn't mind helping, but I don't want to step on any more toes than I feel like I already have. Are you sure my help would be well received?"

"Show up at the gym tomorrow afternoon, and leave the coach to me. It'll all be fine."

Famous last words.

Her bags felt heavier than before as she left the office. She came to Goose Harbor to get away from drama, yet it seemed like she'd just found more. Paige shuffled out of the office, suddenly not looking forward to lugging all her bags home anymore.

Caleb leaned on the lockers across from the main office, his hands jammed in his pockets. Paige kept her head down and walked in the opposite direction from him.

"Wait up." He caught up to her in two strides. "Look, I'm sorry for how I sounded in there. I shouldn't have gotten worked up. Can we talk about this a little more?"

The canvas bag bit into her shoulder, and she switched it to the other arm. "Not if you're just going to tell me no again."

"Let me drive you back to Maggie's."

"What?"

"A ride. To the inn. You have a lot of bags." He rubbed the back of his neck.

She glanced out the front doors. Wind still tickled the trees. Even still, the temperature outside had climbed all day. She'd already considered digging out her bathing suit and heading to the beach later. A ride might not be such a bad idea.

And she and Caleb worked together—she'd have to talk to him again at some point. Might as well get over the awkwardness now while she had the chance.

"Know what? It's hot. I'll take you up on the offer."

He eased both bags from her hands. "I'm parked at the far end of the lot. How about I bring these out to my truck while you wait here? I'll pull up to the front circle." He turned to leave before Paige had a chance to reconsider.

She stood in the lobby and watched him make his way to a large green pickup parked at the back of the lot. Almost everyone had left for the day. The empty school smelled like a mixture of musty old books and industrial strength pine cleaner. Paige pinched the bridge of her nose, fighting the headaches that always plagued her from allergies this time of year.

The woman Bree had pointed out as Amy clipped down the hall toward her on three-inch heels. Her lips were a glossy just-bit-into-a-pomegranate red. A stylish belt with a bejeweled buckle accentuated the woman's trim midsection, and with her blouse unbuttoned at least one button too many, her knotted string of black pearls laid in just the right place to draw even more male attention—as if a woman that stunning needed it.

"You won't last." Amy stopped a few feet away. She crossed her arms over her chest.

"Excuse me?" Paige straightened her spine.

Now probably wasn't the best time to tell Amy she'd be at the volleyball tryouts.

"They haven't been able to keep anyone in that position for years." Amy took a step closer as she eyed Paige from head to toe and found her lacking. The woman towered over her.

Paige focused on the plaque fixed to the wall behind Amy's head. Her father had told her once that fondness might not be within her control, but kindness always was. *Be kind.*

"Thanks for the heads-up." She forced a smile.

"Tell me you've at least taught before."

Paige forced her shoulders and hands to relax, a trick she'd learned over the years from her lawyer father—a master of hiding emotions. *Don't let anyone know they've ruffled your feathers.* "Yes. Three years in Chicago."

Amy laughed and splayed her hand across her ample bosom. "Goose Harbor is completely different than a big city. You won't last. Not with the people in this town and not with that attitude."

Attitude?

Caleb honked the horn of his pickup from the circle drive.

Paige jumped. "I have to go."

Amy trailed her down the front steps. "*You're* with Caleb?"

Whatever that meant.

"Yes." Paige sidestepped Amy to get to the passenger door.

"But—"

She yanked the handle. "Sorry, I really have to leave."

Paige climbed into the cab and buckled her seat belt. She pulled down the visor on the mirror and pretended to check for something in her eye to avoid Caleb's gaze.

Making Amy think she and Caleb were an item probably wasn't her best idea. Besides, why would a guy as handsome as Caleb want to be with someone like Paige? She blinked at her reflection in the mirror: small nose, a dash of brown-sugar freckles on pale cheeks, scrawny arms and drab blond hair—nothing to write home about. Especially not for a guy who looked like he could be one of those rugged hosts on a home-improvement television show.

Not that she cared what Caleb or Amy thought of her. She didn't. Just let her volunteer at Sarah's Home—that's all she wanted from him.

Amy sauntered around the front of Caleb's truck. *Not now.*

He sent Paige a look he hoped told her he was sorry for the delay Amy would, no doubt, cause.

Amy motioned for him to roll down his window. When he did, she leaned on his door and then reached into the car to smooth her hand over an imaginary wrinkle on the sleeve of his shirt. "Running away so quick? Silly man. I didn't get to talk to you today."

Caleb curled his hands around the leather wheel. "You know how it is. The first day is always a whirlwind."

She rested her chin in the palm of her hand and lowered her eyelids halfway when she talked. "We'll have to find some time this week to catch up. Maybe lunch. Or dinner. Or both could be arranged. I could cook for you at my apartment." She played with her necklace.

"We'll see. Have a nice night." Caleb popped the gear out of Park.

Amy crossed her arms and narrowed her eyes when Caleb started to pull away. She shot a mean look at the woman in his passenger seat. Maybe Paige didn't notice.

Amy had to have at least five years on him, not that age mattered that much. She hinted and tried to flirt, and as forward and attractive as she was, most guys would call him insane not to get involved. But he wasn't interested.

How did a guy tell a girl that without hurting her feelings? Besides, it wasn't just her. He wasn't interested in dating anyone. Well, even if he had been open to dating, Amy wouldn't be someone he'd pursue. Too aggressive for his liking, and as far as he knew, she wasn't a Christian.

Caleb puffed out a long stream of air as he pulled out of the parking lot. The local country station blared a sad song over his speakers. Something about a lost dog and a state fair.

Paige crossed her arms and leaned against the passenger door. "I didn't know you were involved with Sarah's Home."

More like stuck with it.

"I am."

He feigned fiddling with the volume control as he stole a glance at Paige. His gut tightened. She was too pretty for her own good. He had to convince her not to go to Sarah's Home. But how?

The truth.

It was time to open up again about Sarah's death. No matter how much he didn't want to. This was his punishment. For the rest of his life he'd relive his failure over and over. He neglected his chance to step in that night to keep Sarah safe, but it was within his power to save Paige.

Chapter Four

Paige glanced across the cab as Caleb pulled onto a road and turned away from the downtown portion of Goose Harbor.

"Where are you taking me?" She tried to keep her voice calm, but she needed to get back to the inn to work on her lesson plan for tomorrow. And do something about this pounding ache in her head. She crossed her arms.

Caleb leaned his elbow on the door frame. "I'm just taking the long way home—that is, if that's okay with you. Like I said back at school, I want to talk."

Okay. She had a lot to get done tonight, but she also needed to smooth things over with Caleb if she was going to be working with him at Sarah's Home.

She nodded once.

Besides, in order to make Goose Harbor her home, she should start getting to know the people here. Of course, she needed to keep her guard up around Caleb. He was a man after all, but she could at least be comfortable enough to be neighborly. Paige didn't know much about him and perhaps now was her chance. Might as well. Between him fixing things at Maggie's, being a teacher in the same hallway as her and now sharing a stake in Sarah's Home, it looked like it would be best to befriend him on some level.

Paige slipped on her sunglasses in order to peek at Caleb without him knowing.

Jane Austen would have described him as dashing, and Paige's favorite author would have been dead right. As the evening sunlight skipped over Caleb's head, the color of his hair seemed to shift from black to brown, brown to black, black to brown. His jaw was all man. Firm and defined, with the slightest bit of cocoa hair lining it. What would he look like clean shaven?

She shifted in her seat.

The man had lost his wife—an irreplaceable woman. Besides that, he had Amy flirting with him, and what man would deny a woman who looked like her? And here Paige was fighting a confusing attraction to him.

Put the brakes on, girl. To stick to her plan she needed to view him like Bryan. Like Dad. Men who cheat and control.

Paige rubbed her temples. Fresh air would help her headache. She rolled down the window. The wind rustled the pages of a small paperback resting on the dash. Paige rescued the book from its precarious place, not wanting the truck to hit a bump and cause it to fall out the window. She glanced at it, thinking the book would be some handyman instructional booklet, but she recognized this cover.

"You're reading *White Fang?*" Somehow the idea of Caleb tucked in an overstuffed chair reading a book didn't fit the image she'd already constructed of him.

"Yeah." He sneaked a glance at her. "It was a favorite when I was younger. I found it the other day in my library and figured it was time for a reread."

"The town library?" She couldn't imagine a town this

small having a good selection, but if the building was well stocked, she needed to check it out.

"No, at my house."

Paige cradled the book on her lap. "You have a library?"

He scratched his brow. "A bedroom full of floor-to-ceiling books—does that count?"

"Sorry. It shouldn't surprise me, but you like to read?"

"A lot. I used to stay up late every night as a kid with a flashlight reading in bed. Although, this book's a bit sadder than I remember—more like real life than I was hoping for when I picked it up."

She fanned her hand over the cover. "True, but after a lot of pain, White Fang does get a happy ending."

It took only a few minutes for the homes to grow farther and farther apart—signaling that they had traveled out of Goose Harbor town boundaries. Caleb turned after a sign that read Dunes State Park and slowly maneuvered the truck as the road snaked around trees. Enough foliage grew in the dunes here to allow for a paved road. Small, different-colored signs marked hiking paths ranging from beginner to expert level. Caleb pulled around the last bend and Paige had to shield her eyes from the sun. They cleared the wooded area and were at the top of a huge dune. Caleb rolled the truck to the edge of the pavement and turned it off.

The view out the windshield made Paige catch her breath. Lake Michigan spilled out before them far into the horizon, its water breaking in a thousand white crests as the water rolled back and forth. A coastline of beaches made up of a mixture of butter-colored sand and patches of long, waving grasses stretched for miles. A small red lighthouse in the distance winked at her. The clouds made a quilt in the sky, woven together with shades of orange, pink and purple as the sun started to sink into the lake.

The knotted feeling in her stomach loosened a bit. She could get used to sights like this. She'd have to remember to come here for her jogs.

"This is beautiful." Paige unbuckled her seat belt and braced her hands on the front of the dash.

Caleb looped his hands over the steering wheel. "It's my favorite spot."

A little girl wearing a bright yellow swimsuit down on the beach ran into the waves laughing. With a bucket in her hand, she scooped up the wet sand and teetered with the effort of hauling it back to where she had been sitting. A man Paige hadn't noticed a moment ago got up and lifted the girl and her bucket into his arms and spun her in a circle. Her giggles echoed up to where Paige and Caleb sat in the truck.

Paige's throat tightened. Why was she being so emotional lately? Something about the pair made her wish for a childhood she never had. *Dad's too busy. He's on another trip. He's working late in the city tonight. He won't be able to give a kiss good-night—maybe tomorrow.*

What would it be like to know joy like that child? To trust that someone would come and not just lighten her load, but lift her up in the process?

Stop dreaming. No more wishing for a life that wouldn't happen. She blinked back the moisture in her eyes.

If the breakup with Bryan had taught her one thing, it was that she was strong. Life had to be what she made it. No more waiting for some white knight that didn't exist.

Her terms. Her control. She didn't need someone to giggle with or to carry her.

Even if it looked like fun.

All right, enough stalling.

Caleb switched his keys from one hand to the other. "I

don't know what Principal Timmons said, but you don't have to volunteer at Sarah's Home." He cringed. That came out wrong.

Paige's gaze—which a moment ago had been fixed out the front window—snapped in his direction. She narrowed her eyes. "What's your problem? Let me guess, you're the type of guy who believes women can't make a difference. We're here just to bat our eyes at you. Is that it?"

"That's not it at all. Listen. The city where Sarah's Home is located—Brookside—it's plagued with home foreclosures and active gangs. Is that really what you want to be dealing with? Some of the students we mentor are gang members. Why mess with danger when there are so many other things you could spend your time doing? Good things, right here in Goose Harbor." Caleb spoke slow and even—it was vital that she understood the level of danger. She needed to back out and never go to Sarah's Home. She should stay locked away. Safe in Goose Harbor. Like Shelby and Maggie.

"Timmons already told me." She pulled a hair tie from her wrist and tucked her hair into a messy bun. "I'll be fine."

"I don't think you get it."

"Actually, I do. And *I think* you're forgetting that not only did I grow up twenty minutes from one of the biggest cities in the country, but I also taught inner-city students. I promise you, Chicago's got more issues than Brookside." She straightened her shoulders, but she was so petite she could never look big and intimidating. No matter how hard she tried. "I'm not afraid."

"You should be." He clenched his jaw.

She tossed her hands in the air. "What's that even supposed to mean? I can't live my life controlled by fear. I won't."

Mayday! The conversation was not going well. He needed to choose his words carefully.

"Did Timmons tell you about my wife?" He paused. "About Sarah?"

"He said she passed away and that she was an incredible woman." Paige's voice was quiet. She studied the floorboard. "I'm sorry for your loss."

"Sarah and I had been friends since grade school." Caleb took a deep breath then continued. "Everyone knew we'd get married." He stared at the window visor and let his vision go fuzzy. Why was he telling her this? Stick to the facts. Don't lose it. But be honest. "I guess you don't need all the backstory."

He looked over at Paige, which was a mistake. Her eyes had gone soft, and she leaned a bit toward him, like she was listening. Like one wounded soldier talking to another, he didn't read pity in her expression. Just that she cared.

She tilted her head. "You don't have to talk about it if you don't want to."

Caleb cleared his throat. "No. I do. See, Sarah had this heart to help others. She wanted to make a difference and didn't care if that put her in danger. I usually went with her when she traveled into Brookside to tutor students. Something about her going alone didn't sit well with me. But then, this one night, we got into a fight. Just yelling. I shouldn't have yelled."

Why? Why did he have to press the issue that night? Caleb asked himself that question every night as he lay in bed. If only he hadn't brought up his desire to start a family—hadn't pushed the issue with Sarah yet again. She'd still be here. Then he could tell her that she was enough for him. He didn't need children. Even if he wanted that life. He'd toss all of those desires in a drawer in order to have Sarah back again.

"We didn't apologize to each other before she left that night." The words tumbled from his mouth like marbles off a table—fast and weighty. "I didn't go with her. I should have. Looking back, I don't know why I didn't just go. She should never have been left on her own there."

The admission felt like fire to his gut. His sister, Shelby, often called him a gentle giant, but when he talked about how he'd failed Sarah, well, then he wanted to punch something. No. Not just something, Caleb wanted to punch himself. After promising to protect his wife for the rest of his life, so quickly he'd failed. Just like he'd failed Mom and Shelby.

God should know better by now than to make him responsible for anyone. Evidently he couldn't handle it.

Paige tentatively laid her hand on his forearm. "You don't have to go on."

Caleb searched her crystal-blue eyes. Did she understand?

Just spit it out. "I got the call three hours later. Some coward attacked her as she was locking up that night. They made off with her purse, her wedding ring and her wallet." He rubbed the butt of his hand against his chest as if the pain could be massaged away. If only. "She died there on the street before the paramedics could start CPR."

Paige squeezed his forearm where her hand still rested. "It's not your fault."

He slipped his arm away from her touch and ran his hand through his hair. The spot on his arm where her hand had been was still warm. "I should have been there."

She shrank back into her side of the truck's cab. "You can't blame yourself."

Enough. He told Paige about Sarah, and there was no reason to dive deeper into his guilt.

Caleb jammed the keys into the ignition and the truck

shook to life. "With the recession, Brookside is even more dangerous than it was when that happened to Sarah. That's why I don't think it's safe for women who aren't from Brookside to be there. The women who live there deal with the danger every single day going about their normal lives, but outsiders just don't get it." He glanced back at her, catching her gaze right before she turned away. "Please reconsider serving at Sarah's Home. That's all I'm asking. There are so many other places you can volunteer that are safer."

Paige's back faced him now as she looked out the window, her eyes locked on Lake Michigan and a little girl and her father playing on the beach.

He glanced over his shoulder and started to back out of the small lot on top of the dune. "Will you at least promise me you'll think about what I said?"

"I promise—to think about it," she whispered. "Thanks for trusting me with your story."

Thankfully, Paige didn't talk again on the way back to Maggie's inn. After telling about Sarah's last day Caleb didn't want to keep up small talk. He hoped Paige understood that.

He turned into the driveway to the inn, and the truck bumped up the gravel road. Someday he'd dig out the roots to some of those big trees so it would be a smoother drive. That, or just pay to have Maggie's driveway cemented.

The second he stopped the truck, Paige unbuckled her seat belt and shot out of the cab like a horse breaking free of a fence. He could only hope her silence had meant that Paige changed her mind about being a part of Sarah's Home. That she was safe now.

Maggie welcomed Paige home for the day with an unexpected hug. "And I have some homemade sun tea waiting for you in the kitchen. Let me just run out to the truck and snag Caleb for a second, and then I'll join you. But feel free to help yourself to some."

Paige pressed through the front door but turned to peek back at Caleb and Maggie as they talked outside of Caleb's truck. Maggie hugged him and swatted at his chest a couple of times while they chatted.

Pulling out her keys, Paige unlocked the door that led to the private living quarters of the inn. She dumped her bags on the desk in her small bedroom and then made her way to the kitchen. Sun tea sounded good. She grabbed a glass and filled it to the top before crossing to the living room. Paige sat in front of the television but didn't turn it on. She took a sip of the tea, then set down the glass and walked over to the bookshelves lining the wall.

Old books were crammed in to fill every available space on the large shelves. Three framed pictures sat on the shelf, as well. One photo off to the side caught her eye. It was a wedding shot—Caleb and a beautiful redheaded bride who must have been Sarah, both with their arms around Maggie.

Paige picked up the picture and studied it. Caleb had such a great smile. If he knew the pain he would go through soon after his wedding, would he still have gone through with it?

Maggie came in balancing a pitcher of tea and a plate of cookies. "I hope you like oatmeal chocolate chip. I know some people prefer raisins in their oatmeal cookies, but I've always thought raisins had no place in dessert. A cookie with raisins is just breakfast in disguise if you ask me."

"Oatmeal chocolate chip is perfect." Paige smiled and snagged two.

"Good." Maggie dropped into an overstuffed side chair and propped her feet up on the coffee table.

Paige sank her teeth into the warm cookie. The chocolate melted on her tongue. "These are delicious. You know, if you want a break in the kitchen I'm still willing to make my special cranberry white-chocolate scones. I'd make them the night before so they'd be ready for guests in the morning."

"Like I said before, I couldn't ask you to do that."

"Sure you could. Maggie, you're letting me live here for free. Making a couple scones is the least I could do."

"If you're sure, then I'll take you up on that next week. I have a doctor's appointment on Thursday so that would work out well." Maggie tossed her feet onto the coffee table. "I hope you don't mind that I just told Caleb he can come do some yard work on Saturday about midmorning. We have no guests booked for the inn on Friday night and that's the first time all summer. But if you don't want the noise and would rather sleep in, I could ask him to come later."

Paige looked back at the shelf that housed the photos of Caleb on his wedding day. "You two are close."

A sad smile played across Maggie's face. "For all intents and purposes he's my brother. You see, he was married to my sister, Sarah. So even though Sarah's gone, he still treats me like I'm his in-law. And hey, if a man's offering free labor around the house, I'm not going to pass it up." Maggie polished off the last cookie.

"I'm so sorry for your loss."

Maggie nodded. "I miss her every day. She was an amazing woman."

In the truck Caleb had told her that Sarah was attacked. But so many questions swirled in Paige's head, still. What had happened to her that she would have needed CPR? "He told me a little about her today."

"Really?" Maggie set down her glass. "He so rarely talks about her. Sometimes it makes me feel like he hasn't processed through everything yet."

"I want to volunteer at Sarah's Home so—"

Maggie popped to her feet and started to pace. "You know he'll never let you, right?"

"How I understand it from Principal Timmons, it's not up to Caleb." Paige crossed her arms and leaned back into the couch cushion.

Maggie stopped moving and faced Paige. "Did he tell you everything?"

Of course not. Men always leave out a bit of the truth. "I don't think so."

She perched on the edge of the coffee table. "My sister was born with a condition that meant one of her legs was longer than the other. She was teased so much at school. You know how cruel kids can be. Well, in the fifth grade she was placed in the same class as Caleb and he heard kids making fun of her and stood up for her. Told them to knock it off. Everyone listened to him because Caleb's always been popular."

Maggie straightened a little owl statue on the shelf. "After that Caleb and Sarah were inseparable. She followed him around and called him her hero. You know, she always said that's why she opened Sarah's Home—because Caleb had saved her and it was her turn to use her time to save others. I think he knows that, and that fact makes what happened even harder for him to deal with it."

Paige nodded. "He blames himself."

"I know. He can be so thickheaded." Maggie shook her head. "But it's ridiculous, and I've told him that a hundred times. He tells himself that if he'd gone along that night,

Sarah would still be alive. But know what I think? I think that the man who shot Sarah could have used his gun on both of them. What does Caleb really think he could have done to fight off a gun?"

Paige gasped. "She was shot?"

"Oh, he didn't tell you that?" Maggie's eyes went wide.

"He only said that she was attacked and died."

"Multiple gunshot wounds. The offender was never found." Maggie looked away, her gazed fixed on the upper part of the wall like it was suddenly the most interesting aspect of the room. A few moments passed before she started speaking again. "I think Caleb has spent the last two years finding every way imaginable to punish himself."

Paige didn't want to press Maggie. After all, Sarah had been her sister. Maggie must have mourned, as well. But it bothered Paige that Caleb felt responsible for everything. "He has to see he's not responsible for the act of a stranger."

Maggie sighed as she picked up the empty plate. "In this world it's a whole lot easier to hold on to guilt than it is to forgive."

"Who does he need to forgive? The gunman?" Paige grabbed the two cups and trailed Maggie into the kitchen.

Maggie laid the dish in the sink and gazed out the window. She pressed her hand to her lips before whispering, "Himself. Caleb needs to forgive himself."

Chapter Five

"Do you want an omelet? I have time to make one. I don't have to pick up Snaggle-Tooth until eight-thirty." Clad in baggy sweats and an old sweatshirt, Shelby leaned against the kitchen cabinets.

Caleb adjusted his tie. His image looked foreign in the hall mirror. He only kept his beard in the summer, but once school officially started, he stayed clean shaven.

He turned and smiled at his little sister. "No, thanks. I'll grab a cup of joe from Cherry Top on the way to school. I wouldn't want to keep you from walking every dog in town," he joked.

She crossed her eyes and stuck out her tongue. "You're impossible, you goof. Well, you better be off—I don't want to keep you from the pretty new teacher."

Ever since he'd made the mistake of casually mentioning his talk with Paige, Shelby found every chance to mention her.

Caleb shoved the large teacher binder into a backpack. "Did I tell you she wants to serve at Sarah's Home?"

"Only about seven times."

"Well, she does." He opened the fridge and grabbed his lunch bag. The rest of the shelves looked bare. "Do you want me to get something on my way home for dinner? I can stop and get groceries if you email me a list."

"You'll be on your own for dinner tonight." Shelby's wavy brown hair fell in front of her eyes as she picked at her nails—a sure sign that she was nervous about something.

Caleb set his bags on the counter. "So you have plans tonight? Going out with one of your girlfriends?"

Shelby bit her lip and looked out the window. "A guy from the singles group is taking me out."

He crossed his arms and fought the papa-bear protective urge rising in his chest. The one that made him want to growl at any man that came within ten feet of her. Shelby was an adult, but she would always be his baby sister.

She'd be married by now if not for the scars on her arms and legs. If he'd listened to her that night when she wanted to talk about their parents' divorce, she wouldn't have been in the church when it went up in flames. She'd be fine now—*whole*. Probably living a full life somewhere besides Goose Harbor, but instead she was stuck here with him. Forever marked.

What did she have to look forward to? Taking care of Caleb and running a small dog-walking business day in and day out couldn't make her happy. He'd asked her to move in with him after Sarah died. The house felt like a museum the months following his wife's funeral. But Shelby deserved better.

She deserved a man who would take care of her who wasn't her brother, but so far all the dates in the past five years had turned and run when they saw the burns on her skin. No wonder she always wore long sleeves and pants.

"Are you sure that's wise?" Caleb kept his voice even. Shelby wouldn't want his pity.

"Settle down, okay? It's dinner, Caleb—not a proposal."

She shoved her hands into the wide pockets on her hooded sweatshirt. "What's your problem anyway? I don't need your approval, nor did I ever ask you to protect me. I can take care of myself."

He gently caught her arm before she could leave the room. "It always starts as dinner and it ends with you hurt." Caleb waited for her to make eye contact. "Just be careful, okay? I don't want you to get your—"

"Hopes up. I know." She pulled away and brushed past him. "Just say it. You don't think someone could like me in that way."

"You know that's not what I meant. I—"

"You're going to be late for work." She jutted a thumb at the large clock on the wall.

He still had twenty minutes before he needed to be in his classroom, but he should leave. A conversation could wait until they had more time. But parting ways with them both worked up didn't sit well with him.

Caleb trailed her out the front door. "Shelby," he called.

She stopped with her hand on the door of her beat-up Volkswagen. With her back to him, her shoulders sagged.

He stepped closer and laid a hand on her shoulder. "I love you."

"I know," she whispered.

"I don't want to see you hurt again." Why wouldn't she look at him?

She took in a deep breath and blinked rapidly. "You can't protect me forever. You know that, right?"

"A brother can sure try." Caleb leaned forward and kissed the top of her head. "Have a good day."

He climbed into his truck and backed out of their driveway. Books, besides *White Fang,* which he had finished last night, scattered across the floor of the passenger side. Paige must have left one of her bags yesterday. He didn't want her to waste time searching frantically for those at Maggie's. Coffee from Cherry Top would have to wait until the next school day.

Usually the sunshine on Lake Michigan kept his attention during his drive, but this morning he kept thinking about the sad expression on Shelby's face.

Wanting solitude, he snapped off the radio dial.

You can't protect me forever. It wasn't the first time she'd tossed those words at him. Maggie also warned him over and over to leave Shelby alone and let her make her own mistakes. But surely it wasn't wrong to shelter people in your life from pain? Yes, his protective urge had doubled since Sarah's death. But this world was dangerous. It didn't help that his best friend was a cop and told him terrible stories of things that happened to people—real people. All of it showed Caleb that he had to protect the people he loved or risk losing them.

"God, have I been wrong all along? Is it so bad to try to protect the people I love? Isn't that what You did for us on the cross?"

It all came down to trust. Did Caleb trust God? Of course he did—but that same God let Sarah die. Sometimes, a man had to take protection into his own hands because God couldn't stop a criminal bent on causing pain.

Caleb shook his head as he pulled out of his neighborhood.

Nothing made sense anymore.

Up way before her alarm, Paige cradled a cup of iced tea as she gazed out the window and tried to mentally prepare herself for the first day of school. Outside, the sun burned on the eastern horizon. Primrose hues reached like slender fingers up over the sand dunes, the pink mingling high up into the purple velvet sky.

Paige commanded the butterflies in her stomach to die. Freshmen were supposed to have first-day-of-school jitters. Not teachers.

Her Bible rested on her nightstand where she'd set it when she finished unpacking last night. She scooped it up and fumbled through the still-crisp pages. This was the part she didn't enjoy. The people at her old church told her she should read every day, but she never understood just how, because choosing what to read felt like playing a game of pin-the-tail-on-the-donkey.

Should she just open the book at random and let God show her what He wanted? That never seemed to work. Start at the beginning? Except that one book—Numbers— always made her brain hurt. Reading it made no sense. Some of her friends back in Chicago seemed to find a daily message just waiting for them in the Scriptures, but to her the book was a locked treasure chest with no key. That—and it said she should submit to men.

Right.

She set the Bible back down.

A buzzer sounded in the kitchen, which meant Maggie was up preparing breakfast for her guests. Paige ran a comb through her hair one last time and swiped some gloss over her lips. Done. She might as well head to the high school early and finish last-minute preparations before the students filed in. Paige grabbed the canvas bag full of books and stepped out of her room. She should have one more bag, but she realized late last night that she'd left the second bag in Caleb's truck.

"Well, hi there, dear." Ida scooted a stack of pancakes onto an empty platter. "Would you care for one? I made them myself. Secret recipe and all." She winked.

Paige set her bag of books on the counter. "You know, I actually have an extra couple minutes. I might as well."

All the dishes in the sink had been rinsed and the room smelled like the lemon all-purpose spray Maggie used on the counters. Although, when Maggie cooked, the place usually looked like someone had waged a food fight in the room. She never cleaned until long after breakfast service.

"Where's Maggie?"

Ida tottered over with two pancakes arranged on a delft-blue plate. "She's not feeling well this morning so I took over for her."

Paige set down her fork. "She's sick? Oh, no, I hope it's not bad. Should I do something? Do you need help?" Not that she had time this morning, but Maggie had let her stay here for free.

"You just keep that seat and eat for me. Nothing makes me happier than people eating my cooking." Ida fiddled with the coffeemaker.

Paige dumped warm maple syrup all over her plate.

Ida continued, "That is, except for love. Love makes me happier than just about anything else in the world. But then, you knew that."

Paige tried to force a smile. Ida could enjoy her rosy version of love. But Paige knew better. Men worth sighing over existed in two places—books and the olden days when Ida found her husband. But men weren't like that anymore. Love led to pain. End of story. No need to pop Ida's sweet soap bubble, though.

Ida arranged tiny mugs onto the coffee cart. "You know, that's Magpie's real problem. If she could just find a man to love I think she'd be a lot happier."

Right. Like marrying Dad had made Mom so much cheerier. Especially when Mom discovered how many years Dad had been cheating on her. Why had she stayed with him, anyway?

No longer hungry, Paige pushed her plate a few inches

away. "It could be dangerous to use whether or not someone has a man in her life as a basis for measuring happiness. A lot of women are perfectly capable of taking care of themselves."

"Oh, I'm not saying that at all. No one needs a man to be whole. If they're looking for a man to do that—" Ida giggled "—tough cookies. They're damaged goods just like the rest of us. No man can meet that need, I'm afraid. Only the good Lord is up for that task. But I know Maggie's heart—she longs for a family. The Lord put that desire inside of her, and He'll meet that in good time."

Of course—just like God had met her dream of a family and a faithful husband.

Wasn't going to happen.

God was too busy managing the important functions of the world. Starving people, countries at war and natural disasters ranked much higher on His list.

Paige stretched her fingers, willing her muscles to relax. *Don't get worked up.* One little old lady spouting off foolishness shouldn't ruin her day. *Smile and nod to Ida and be done with this conversation.*

But Paige's mouth didn't obey. "Hasn't Maggie lived here her whole life? I'm guessing she knows all the men in town. I could be wrong, but her odds of finding someone now are pretty slim."

Ida pressed her hands over her heart. "God will send her someone—a man who's just right. For you, too. But you must make time for love, dear."

Enough. "No offense, but I'm not really looking for that sort of thing." Paige pulled her plate closer and started eating again.

Ida squinted and shuffled forward. "Are you not sleeping well? You look a mite tired."

Great. Did she have bags under her eyes?

She'd been up so late last night thinking after she received an email from Mom saying they'd already received an offer on the house. Paige's childhood home—gone that quickly. Now she'd have to find a free weekend to pick up her belongings because she definitely didn't want her mom to choose what was worth keeping and what she should toss.

"I just have a lot on my mind with school starting. Besides, the last six months of my life have been a mess."

"You know, we're all in the middle of a mess. That's just life, girl. If you're waiting for a cleanup crew, well, they're simply not coming." She patted Paige's arm. "Now, look at that—we're talking about good men and here Caleb turns up. He's one I'd keep my heart open to if I was you." Ida motioned toward the window.

"No, thanks." Paige smiled at the well-meaning old woman. Even still, she peeked out the window to watch the man in question stroll across the yard.

Caleb stepped through the back door into the kitchen. He'd shaved since last night, and it made him even more attractive, if that was possible. Without his beard, he'd shed the mountain-man vibe. Now, with his strong jawline, he looked like a powerful businessman ready to take on the world. He wore the go-to man uniform of khakis and a blue oxford. She noticed a cleft in his chin à la Ben Affleck. Why would he ever hide that behind a beard?

"Morning," she offered. "Maggie's sick if you're looking for her."

"Actually, I'm looking for you."

"For me?" Paige's pulse zinged into hyperdrive. She took in air at the wrong time and started to choke on her bite of pancake.

He wore a boyish smile. "Need the Heimlich?"

"I'm okay." She gulped down the rest of her water as heat crawled up the back of her neck.

Caleb had an effect on her that she couldn't deny. Maybe it was because he saw her that first day, so distraught, and treated her with kindness and respect when she fell to pieces. It could be because he'd shared honestly about his wife when she didn't need all the details—even if his fear from that incident put them at odds over her position at Sarah's Home. Perhaps her attraction hinged on all the praise she'd heard about him around town or seeing him interact with kids of all ages over the past few days. The man definitely had a paternal drive. Maggie went on about how wonderful he was. Ida did, too. So did the store clerk at the mom-and-pop convenience store.

Or the feeling could have nothing to do with any of that.

Mischief danced behind Caleb's expression. Looking into his eyes was oddly comfortable, like snuggling by a warm fire on a winter's night. A sudden desire to lean closer to him overwhelmed her.

And he was only inches away....

Paige rocked back in her seat, breaking eye contact.

Whoa. Let's not go off the deep end about a guy. Making up her mind too soon about a man had caused trouble in the past. Whatever the reason for the feelings swirling in her heart, the draw needed to go away. Jay, Tommy and Bryan had all seemed nice at first, too. It looked like it was time to put her internal junkyard dog back on patrol around her heart.

Caleb set his keys on the counter but they fell onto the floor. An out-of-character chuckle left his lips and he grabbed them from the tiles. "You left your books in my truck. I thought you might need them."

"Oh, thanks." Real eloquent.

"Do you want a ride?"

"Um, sure." Paige slid off her stool and squeezed past Caleb to get to the sink with her dirty plate. She couldn't help breathing in his cologne.

Paige paused near him for a moment. Whatever cologne he wore had a sweet, woodsy smell with a mix of vanilla.

Back at home, her mother had a cedar chest in the master bedroom that she stored a fur coat in. In grade school, Paige used to love to sit next to the chest and talk to Mom while she got ready for the day. That smell always calmed her, as if her body knew it meant safety and home.

Caleb smelled like that.

She shook her head. *Rinse off the dish already.*

After placing the plate in the dishwasher, Paige waved to Ida and then followed Caleb out to the truck. He wordlessly hoisted her bags into the truck's bed. An awkward silence filled the cab on the drive to the school—no radio, no windows down, no talking.

Paige watched him out of the corner of her eye as he parked in the school's staff lot. After he shared about Sarah yesterday, she had felt a connection to him. Caleb and she might not see eye to eye on Sarah's Home, but she had to admit, he was sweet to try to protect her. He didn't even know her, and he already wanted to make sure she was safe.

No. That's controlling. And not healthy. Just another Bryan in the making.

She crossed her arms. Somehow in a matter of days, Caleb had worked his way into her heart. That needed to stop.

She tightened the hold on her bag.

As they walked through the hallway students waved at Caleb and a couple of guys exchanged high fives with him. A group of teens started to clap when they passed.

"Mr. Beck, I have you for fourth period. Can we play that game in study hall again?"

"We'll talk about it then." Caleb laughed and stopped to joke with some of the students.

Paige kept walking. She should focus her attention on going over her lesson plan one last time and not on how good Caleb Beck looked clean shaven, how he smelled like home, or how much the people in this town loved him.

All those thoughts were far too dangerous.

"All right." Caleb stepped away from the podium in front of his classroom. The students sat in pairs behind large black lab tables. He breathed a silent prayer that what he taught them in class would reveal God to them in tangible ways. Goose Harbor High was a public school, but Caleb believed all truth pointed to God.

"I know that bell's going to ring and you all want to head home, but humor me for these last few minutes. Let's brainstorm a list of ways science is part of our daily lives." He rolled up his sleeve and grabbed a marker for the whiteboard. "Think of ways that science influenced something you did over the summer."

"Can you give us an example?" A boy yawned in the back row.

Caleb set down the marker and instead pulled up a stool and sat down. "Sure. Here's one. I had a camping trip planned over the Fourth of July, but as you all probably remember, we had rain that flooded the area. So, because of the weather I had to change my plans. That's science. Those cell phones you're all texting on behind your desks as if you don't think I notice—that's science, too. The technology."

A couple of students looked up from their phones.

"How about when my mom burned my breakfast this

morning so I had to grab a Pop-Tart on the way out the door?" The boy in the back row grinned.

Caleb nodded. "Science."

"I made out with a girl at summer camp and got mono," another student offered.

The class erupted in laughter.

"Science…and hopefully lesson learned." Caleb stood as the bell sounded. Students grabbed their bags and started to make for the door. "We'll talk more about this next time, but for tonight everyone write a paragraph about how science affected you in some way this past week."

Caleb stuffed papers into his messenger bag and locked up his room. Normally he'd stay around for an hour after school in case a student wanted to talk, but no one would need help on the first day. Besides, tonight some of the volunteers at Sarah's Home were meeting to clean up the building and get it ready for the nonprofit to open its doors for the school season.

Caleb took calculated steps down the hall, because he knew he'd have to walk past Amy's office. For everything in the world, he didn't want his boots to squeak on the linoleum floor as he passed by her. Just after her thirty-fifth birthday it seemed like the primal instinct to marry had overpowered her rational work behavior. Caleb couldn't put his finger on it, but somewhere along the line Amy decided that he was the man for her. The other guys mocked him unmercifully. They harped on the fact that Amy had years on him and consequently dubbed him "cougar bait."

He hated it all. Hated how embarrassed he got, and hated that she didn't pick up on any of his hints. A lot of men would have considered her attractive. Gorgeous, even. He wasn't blind, just not interested.

His shoe caught on a rug between doorways and made a thumping flat tire sound. It was instantly followed by the *click, click, click* of high heels. Caleb released a hiss of breath and shot up a quick prayer for patience.

"Hey there, handsome!" She wore all red today. Red, tailored suit coat with matching pencil skirt and even redder pumps. Her was face made up, her hair curled and fixed in place. Amy was the kind of woman who was always chomping on gum.

"Why didn't you stop in and say hi?" she gushed, her hand cupping his elbow. "Oh, no! Caleb, you have marker on your shirt." She ran her hands up his arms and down his chest, pretending to check for more. "If you want I can wash it for you. I know just the thing to get out a stain like that." She rested both hands on his chest, a look of concern plastered on her upturned face.

Just then, Paige and Bree walked by. They both looked right at Amy's hands resting on him. Why now? For some reason Paige's opinion mattered. She'd been the first person to go toe-to-toe with him in the past two years. His friends in Goose Harbor had coddled him after what happened to Sarah. Hopefully Paige wouldn't do the same now that she knew the details.

What must she think of his exchange with Amy? Caleb sure didn't want any of the women thinking he was willing to lead Amy on.

He stepped back, took Amy's wrists and set her hands back alongside her body. "It'll wash out."

"Oh, don't mind me. I'm just trying to help a clueless bachelor." Amy leaned toward him, lips puckered.

"Widower." He took a deep breath. *Be kind.* "Anyway, thanks for the offer, but I have Shelby if I need help. Speaking of which, I actually have to head home. You have a great evening."

He ducked out of her reach and kept his head down until he arrived at the parking lot. Caleb sank into the driver's seat and rubbed his thumbs back and forth over the steering wheel. Should he go back in and find Paige, offer her a ride home again? He'd have to invent a reason....

He put the truck in Reverse but still scanned the lot for a woman with blond hair.

Not outside. Maybe she already left.

Just go home.

Life had become so predictable over the past two years—go to work, go to church, take care of Maggie and Shelby, avoid Amy, try to manage Sarah's Home—but suddenly Caleb itched for a change.

Chapter Six

Paige hunkered into the seat between Amy and Principal Timmons. Amy narrowed her eyes at Paige and flared her nostrils like it took her every ounce of effort not to start screaming. Her bloodred nails pounded against the table.

Amy leaned closer and in a harsh whisper said, "Exactly what are you doing here?"

If Principal Timmons heard her, he didn't let on.

Paige gulped. "Only helping today with tryouts."

"You mean trying to steal another one of my jobs?"

"I didn't—"

Amy grabbed her clipboard and rounded the table to face the girls waiting to try out. "There will be two fifteen-minute scrimmage matches and then we'll be done. Make sure your number is fixed to your back and that it matches the form you filled out. There will be three of us walking around taking notes and weighing in on who will make the team this year, so don't come crying to me if you don't make the list."

Timmons nudged Paige, his eyebrows raised as if to say, *see*.

Amy split the girls into teams and blew her whistle to signal the start of the first match. All three judges paced around the gym. Paige carried a pad of paper and scribbled notes, praying she made the right choices. Making the team had meant so much to her in high school and college. But a few of these girls wouldn't feel that elation; instead, they'd rush to the team posting next week and leave in tears. She didn't like thinking about that aspect of the responsibility.

At the end of tryouts, Paige handed her notes to the principal. "That's it, then."

He scanned her ranking of the girls and nodded. "Thank you for taking part in this on such short notice. I appreciate your input." Timmons tucked the papers away. "Do you need directions to get to Sarah's Home tonight?"

She paused. "Sarah's Home—has it opened already? Why didn't I hear anything?"

Timmons shoved his hands in his suit coat pockets. "Caleb sent an email out about meeting tonight to clean the building since it's been locked for most of the summer. So I guess that means you're not on the mailing list yet."

Paige fisted her hands. She wanted to shake Caleb for not telling her. Oh, he'd hear about this when she saw him later. Only earlier today she'd considered him such a nice guy, so much that she'd warned herself not to be attracted to him.

What a joke.

He knew she wanted to be involved and hadn't said a word when he drove her to school that morning. The nerve of that man! He had the whole look-like-the-innocent-sheep-but-be-the-tick-on-it act down—or something.

She pulled up the notes app on her phone and entered in the time and directions to Sarah's Home from Principal Timmons and assured him she could drive there herself.

Lenny the Leech sat on a plastic chair with his legs propped up near the main entrance. Not what she wanted to deal with right now. On edge because Caleb didn't tell her about the gathering tonight, she might snap at poor Lenny for nothing other than him being there. Paige wanted to go home, change and have an hour to unwind before heading to Brookside. Her temper needed to dissipate before she arrived at Sarah's Home. If only she had time for a jog. Not today.

She veered toward the doors that led back into the school hallways; she'd just take the long way out and avoid Lenny altogether.

"Miss Windom!" A girl with a long black braid chased after her. When Paige stopped and turned back around, the girl puffed as she caught her breath. "I'm Tammie. I'm in your second period class."

"I remember you." Paige smiled. The girl had raised her hand to answer almost every question. She'd also aced the quiz on the books covered in the school's required summer reading program.

"I just wanted to tell you that I loved what you said about that Robert Frost poem. I've been thinking about it all day, and I think you've helped me choose what to do after graduation." Tammie jumped up and down.

Paige's eyes went wide. "Really?" Teaching always amazed her. The impact she could have through words without even realizing it was happening made her want to rethink everything she said and did. Once a teacher, students watched her actions. She needed to remember that.

"Yeah, that thing about taking the less-traveled path, it finally helped me make the decision to go on a long-term mission trip after graduation instead of going straight to college. I've been wanting to but was never brave enough to actually say it. I called my parents after school and they're totally supportive. I don't know what I was so afraid of, after all." She lunged to hug Paige.

Paige laughed and hugged her back, welcoming the human contact. "I'm glad it was helpful."

"You're cool, Miss W." Tammie flipped her hair over her shoulder. "I'm glad they picked you for the position."

"Me, too." Paige winked at her.

Tammie hugged a textbook to her stomach. "Okay, but there's one more thing. Are you going to the Barn Dance?"

No, because a raccoon with rabies could best her on the dance floor. "I haven't heard anything about a Barn Dance."

"It's tradition. At the end of the first month of class, the school holds the annual Barn Dance, and the teachers chaperone it. Tell me you'll be there. I don't like to do stuff like that, but if you go, I'll go."

"Well." Paige looped her hand on her bag strap. "How about I promise to think about it?"

"Okay, but if that's the case, then I promise to hound you about it every day until you say you're going." Tammie walked backward down the hall so she was still facing Paige.

"Deal." Paige shook her head good-naturedly. Hopefully Tammie would forget to badger her about the dance, and Paige wouldn't have to find an excuse to not go.

After leaving home, Paige made a promise to herself to learn new things. Despite the few years she'd worked in the inner city, for the most part Paige had grown up sheltered and with so many chores taken care of by hired help. Cooking and cleaning were high on her must-learn list. Dancing, however, was not.

Tammie joined her friends and left while Paige gathered her bags again and headed for the side entrance. Amy fell into step beside her. Where did she even come from?

"I see everyone just loves the new teacher. A word of advice? Don't let it go to your head." Amy placed her hand on the door handle so Paige couldn't leave. "Just a hint, Paige. If you were trying to get anywhere with Caleb, it's not going to happen. It would really be best if you kept your distance from him."

She didn't care about Caleb, but Amy didn't know that. This woman needed to realize that it wasn't okay to push other people around. Amy had done just that to all the girls at volleyball tryouts, but she wasn't about to get away with treating Paige that way.

"What's that even supposed to mean? You can't go around threatening people." Paige's hands popped to her hips making the straps on her bags dig into her shoulders. Hard. Amy didn't answer her. She lifted her hand off the door handle and walked off down the hallway.

Oh! Paige would have loved to say something to get under Amy's skin. But she didn't know Caleb well enough to know if he enjoyed the attention from Amy. In the truck after the teacher's institute he'd seemed annoyed when Amy flirted with him. Then again, Paige's record at judging men was not the greatest.

Either way, Amy could have Caleb because Paige sure didn't want him.

The ride to Brookside took a solid thirty-five minutes. Quaint shoreline towns and winding roads near the dunes gave way to flat-grid neighborhoods and then a sprawling downtown. The economic difference from the tourist section to the normal towns in the state shocked her.

After passing the Welcome to Brookside sign, Paige drove by empty lots, weaved around trash in the street and gawked at the boarded-up homes and warehouses. The condition was far worse than the part of Chicago where she taught last year. Brookside looked like it was dying.

A crumbling concrete lot made up the area in front of

Sarah's Home. Weeds grew knee-high through the cracks near the sidewalk. Shouldn't someone cut those? A single light flickered on the front of the building and only illuminated half of the nonprofit's sign. Chills washed down Paige's back. Maybe this had all been a mistake.

Maybe Caleb was right.

No, he couldn't be. Mistake or not, she'd go in. If only to prove Caleb Beck wrong and show one more man that he couldn't call the shots in her life.

Five other cars, including Caleb's truck, filled the lot. Paige sucked in a deep, fortifying breath and left her car. She checked the door handle to make certain her Mazda was locked and then headed into the building.

The tight feeling in her lungs went away the second she stepped inside. Fresh paint in bright colors filled the first few rooms. There were tables and desks to work at, a room with five old computers, and another with science equipment. Inside felt like a safe haven in the midst of the darkness shadowing Brookside.

She followed the sound of voices to the back dining room where everyone huddled around a table over bowls of pasta. The room fell silent when she stepped through the doorway.

Caleb's mouth hung open and his fork stopped midair. "What are you doing here?"

Great. Now she'd been asked that same question twice today.

"I'm here to help." Paige shrugged.

Caleb rose and crossed to where she stood. His brows formed a deep V. "I thought we talked about this." His voice held an insistent tone.

Paige tugged a hair tie from her wrist and tossed her hair into a messy bun, then she leaned to look around him at everyone else. Did he really want to get into a heated conversation in front of the other volunteers?

Principal Timmons motioned for everyone to bring their bowls to the large kitchen sink. "I think it's about time we start working. Marty and Sam, you've got the floors. Vick and Claire, you have the bathrooms, and please also make a list of supplies that need to be restocked. I'll be in the office or the basement with Wayne. Smalls—" he pointed at a teenage boy wearing orange high-tops and boasting what looked like the beginning of a patchy mustache "—you can wash up these dishes. But before we get started, I'd like to introduce Paige Windom. Paige is the woman I told you about at our last board meeting, and she's going to be a great asset to our team. She's come all the way from Chicago to help us." Timmons offered an encouraging smile. "Paige, we'd love to hear your ideas about ways to improve Sarah's Home."

"Now?" Paige's voice squeaked. Her gaze darted to Caleb. He looked like a bull about to start pawing the ground.

Timmons didn't seem to notice. "If you have any ideas now, we'd love to hear them. The board's made up of Marty, Claire and myself, and we could all head to the office if you'd like."

Paige clutched her purse, suddenly feeling inadequate. "Maybe we should wait until after I've been here a few weeks." These people were looking at her like she had a special plan to save their nonprofit when the truth was, she didn't even know what was wrong with it. She'd left her life back in Chicago thinking Sarah's Home would save her. It was disheartening to find out the place she'd depended on for redirection needed rescuing instead.

Everyone but Smalls and Caleb dispersed to their assigned tasks. Smalls whistled long and low. "You're a fine-looking lady. I wouldn't mind—"

Caleb grimaced. "Be respectful."

Smalls stood a bit straighter, although it was hard to tell with his baggy pants. "Apologies. I mean, you're one pretty woman, Miss Windom."

Paige laughed. "Thanks. I think. But you can just call me Paige." She sidestepped Caleb and placed her purse on the counter. "Nice shoes. Very bright."

"You like them? Orange beats all." The boy's chest puffed out like she'd just given him the best compliment.

"Could you use some help with those dishes?"

Caleb stayed rooted in the same spot. He worked his jaw back and forth like he wanted to say something, but fought the urge.

Smalls motioned for her to join him at the deep, industrial sinks. He nudged her as she rolled up her sleeves. "See how I did that? I'm a player. Got you to come do my work."

"Between you and me, you still have a lot to learn about women." Paige smiled at the teenager. His forced charm, seasoned with street smarts, had a way of softening her heart and made Paige miss her Chicago students.

"Aww, haters gonna hate." He grabbed the scrub brush and laughed.

"So, you volunteer here?" Paige tried to ignore Caleb looming in the doorway. *Go do something.*

"Kind of. More like, they can't shake me even if they want to." Smalls grinned, showing a chipped front tooth. "Timmons said you're from Chicago—that right?"

Paige plunged her hands into the lukewarm water and fished out the tattered rag. "I'm from the suburbs outside of the city, but I taught there for a few years."

"Chicago's off the hiz-zay." He said it like it was two

words, his voice getting louder on the last part. "I'd give everything to go there."

"Let me guess—for the deep-dish pizza?" Paige glanced behind her. Thankfully Caleb had left at some point during her conversation with Smalls.

Smalls started drying off the plates. "Naw, man. Keep up. Chicago's the home of slam poetry."

"You do slam poetry?" She'd gone to a slam contest before, where poets competed against one another—rattling off poems they made up. A couple of the well-known improv theaters in Chicago hosted slam poetry events. She'd enjoyed attending them and marveled at people who could come up with intelligent work on the spot.

"Sometimes." Smalls shrugged. "There's a place on the west side of town that does it once a month. I'm not so bad at it."

Paige rinsed off the last bowl. "I'd love to come see you sometime."

"Really? You'd do that?" Smalls broke into a huge, genuine smile.

"Sure."

After Paige and Smalls finished the dishes, they went to the basement and scrubbed shelves and helped Vick and Claire compile a supply list. She learned that Claire was a retired cop from Brookside who specialized in the juvenile division while on the force. She was also the only other woman, besides Paige, currently serving at the nonprofit.

At the end of the night everyone gathered in the kitchen. Timmons offered her his chair.

Marty, an aging man who looked like he might have been the leader of a motorcycle gang at some point, cleared his throat. "I wanted to thank everyone for their hard work tonight. It looks like we'll be shining for our opening next week. Please remember we've moved our open night from

Tuesday to Thursday this year. Unless anyone else has something to say, let's head out. We'll see you all next week."

Paige hoped to catch a couple of the people she hadn't gotten to visit with yet, but then realized that wasn't going to happen. At past nine on a school night, everyone at Sarah's Home seemed to want leave right away. She grabbed her purse and almost made it out the door before remembering she'd brought a coat. Where did she leave it? Paige turned back down the hallway and took the stairs to the basement two at a time. Her coat wasn't downstairs, either. No matter, she'd be here next week and find it then. But now, the muscles in her back ached, and she just wanted to get back to Maggie's inn, take off her shoes and relax. It had been a long day.

Caleb's truck was parked next to her compact car, but besides that everyone had already left. She clicked the button to unlock her Mazda then froze. Someone waited in the space between her car and Caleb's truck, right outside her driver's door. A scream died on Paige's lips. She never could find her voice when scared.

"Are you really set on being a part of this?" *Caleb.* Only Caleb. She should have known. A man's voice had never sounded so good.

Her knees stopped wobbling.

She loosened the hold on her purse. "You know, you really shouldn't hide behind dark trucks and scare women. I could have maced you."

He crossed his arms and leaned against her car. "At least you're admitting there's something to be afraid of."

Paige blew her bangs out of her eyes. "Yeah. Creepy science teachers who huddle by my car."

Caleb's hands dropped to his sides. "I wasn't huddling."

"You kind of were."

"It's cold outside and—wait, you made me lose my train of thought." He took a step closer to her. Close enough she could see his eyelashes; they were long for a man. She'd love to have lashes like that.

Despite the warm temperatures during the day, the evening had chilled. Crisp puffs of breath escaped from both of their lips and vanished into the air. The streetlight in front of Sarah's Home flickered three times before going out completely. Darkness almost cloaked a homeless man crouched near the doorway of a boarded-up store across the street. A police siren echoed in the distance, and down the block a man slammed a car door and started to yell at someone.

Paige shivered. From cold. Or the reality of Brookside. She couldn't tell.

Caleb tilted his head. What must he be thinking?

"After tonight. After actually seeing this place…do you still want to be involved?" He spoke so quietly, she had to lean even closer.

Did she? Paige bit her lip. "Yes. Of course." If only to prove she could.

"But I don't understand. You've now—"

"Listen, because of Principal Timmons, my dad has been involved with this place from the start. We've received every newsletter you sent. I used to scour the mail for them. I always wanted to be a teacher, but Sarah's Home opened my mind to helping students outside of my comfort zone. Because of those newsletters I changed the entire course of my education—helping students like the ones that come here became my passion. You don't just back down from something you've thought about for years." Paige tried to keep the quiver out of her voice.

Caleb brought one of his hands to his mouth and took another loud, deep breath. "It's not safe, Paige. Don't you see that?" He braced one hand on her car and one hand on his truck. "For instance, tonight—what if I hadn't stayed and made sure you got to your car safely?"

Defuse the situation. "Then you wouldn't have been hiding by it?"

He tipped his head back and looked up at the sky for a moment. "Be serious. This is a dangerous city."

"So you keep saying." Oh, she just wanted to get in her car and go home.

He shoved his hands into his pockets. "I'll continue to remind you of that until you get it."

Enough. Paige folded her arms, pressing her hands into her armpits to hide that they were shaking. "And what exactly does *getting it* mean? Dropping out? Not being a part of this? You know, why are guys like this?"

"Like what?"

She took a step closer to him. "Just because you don't agree with something, doesn't mean you can bully me until—"

"I'm not bullying you." He put his hands on her shoulders, making her look up at him.

"You are." The words should have come out with more force and in a more convincing tone, but some of her fight was gone. Speaking up was harder than she imagined. No wonder she'd never been able to state her feelings with Bryan. It was tiring to disagree with someone, and he wouldn't have let the conversation go on this long if she'd tried.

Paige swallowed hard. Caleb's chocolate gaze locked with hers, full of questions she didn't have answers to. The pressure of his hands on her shoulders wasn't forceful. Not like he wanted to stop her from talking. Instead, they felt comforting and reassuring in a way that didn't make sense. With his eyes he asked her to keep talking—

to let him in on whatever secret formed this wall of tension between them.

She opened her mouth. Then closed it.

No. She couldn't tell him about Bryan, Jay and Tommy. And definitely not about Dad. A man like Caleb wouldn't care to hear about the ribbons of betrayal that each past relationship had woven into the fabric of her heart. So much that the ribbons were all she could see—all she knew about herself. Paige—the woman men don't stay with.

Suddenly, Caleb turned and placed both hands on his truck. He bowed his head and his eyes snapped shut.

"What are you doing?" She missed the warmth of his hands. It was cold out, after all.

Eyes still closed, Caleb sighed. "Praying. I'm praying." After a few minutes of silence, he straightened. "You're cold."

In a fluid movement, he unsnapped his jacket and slipped it around her shoulders. As he buttoned the first two clasps, a waft of his warmth and scent rushed over her. It was masculine, a perfect mixture of pine trees and fresh night rain and hard work.

Paige reached to unsnap the coat. "It's not necessary… my car will warm up and—"

Caleb cupped his hands over hers. Paige froze.

"Please keep the coat on." Caleb's voice was gentle. "You can give it back to me tomorrow."

She kept staring into his eyes. As much as she wanted to fight against Caleb and believe he was just another controlling man, Paige couldn't deny the concern written in his wrinkled brow and open expression.

"I might forget it tomorrow. Let me just—"

Still holding her hands, Caleb leaned a little closer. "Goose Harbor's a small town. I'm fairly certain we'll cross paths again." He let go and clicked the button to unlock his truck. "Be safe, Paige."

She nodded and fumbled with her keys as she got into her Mazda. Her engine coughed when she turned it on, and she slowly pulled out of the parking lot. Caleb's truck followed. When she had a bit more money, she'd have to have her car tuned up. What would she do if it broke down in Brookside? Phone AAA and wait by the side of the road? Creepy.

At the stop sign she glanced at the truck lights behind her in the rearview mirror. *Caleb*. He'd take care of her if the Mazda broke down tonight.

For the first time in a long time, Paige was thankful for the protection of a man.

Chapter Seven

Don't look for her.

He'd checked already and she wasn't at the farmer's market. Besides, Paige Windom certainly didn't need him watching out for her, nor did she seem to want it. Nevertheless, she was on his mind this morning. No thanks to Shelby, who teased him mercilessly the whole walk to the square.

Is that girl you keep talking about going to be here? Paige? She's pretty, isn't she? Don't argue with me, Caleb. You're a goner for her. I know because you talk about her every day at dinner.

Between Shelby and Maggie, suddenly every female in his life had turned into a matchmaker.

Caleb pulled his wallet out of his back pocket and paid for the produce Shelby picked out from Farmer Turner's booth at the weekly farmer's market. The prices always seemed high to him, but because of Goose Harbor's local ordinance against chain stores within city limits, the closest grocery store was more than a twenty-minute drive away. That alone made the farmer's market that took over the square each Saturday morning a staple for most of the population.

He grabbed the canvas bag from Farmer Turner and searched the small crowd in the square for his sister. Shelby chatted near the gazebo with Mrs. Clarkson, the old widow who the year-round residents in town made a point to look out for. High-school boys shoveled the Clarkson homestead driveway without being asked. The postman stopped in, and she'd ask him to reach a cobweb on the ceiling. Goose Harbor even hosted an annual event dubbed The Orphaned Sock Mixer, where everyone donated socks without a mate to Mrs. Clarkson, who sewed them into the oddest sweatshirt-like garments. It had turned into a huge potluck event that everyone looked forward to after the tourist season died down.

Goose Harbor might be a strange town, but it was home and it was safe and the couple of people left in the world that he loved could live protected here. He didn't have to worry about Maggie getting taken advantage of in her business or Shelby being hurt by some man he didn't know. Not as long as they stayed in town, where the year-round residents knew them and their past hurts, and sheltered them.

Across the grassy town square, near the small rose garden, Principal Timmons sat on a park bench and waved for Caleb to join him. Yes, then there was the bad side of small-town living—he could never escape his boss. Good thing he liked the man.

Timmons held a giant mint chocolate-chip ice-cream cone as he smiled at Caleb. "Enjoying your first school-year weekend?"

"Plan to." Caleb set the heavy canvas bag next to Timmons. "Did you need something?"

"I know we're off school hours, but I wanted to remind you about the Barn Dance. I should have done so on Friday, but I forgot."

His gut tightened. "What about the Barn Dance?"

Out of all of Goose Harbor's yearly festivals—and there were many—the Barn Dance had been Sarah's favorite. The students loved the event and most of the teachers and school staff attended, but there was always a scramble to find adults willing to wear the label of chaperone. It probably had something to do with the fact that the chaperones had to serve as square-dance instructors for the party, as well. Caleb avoided the event the past two years. Even drove out of town so he wouldn't have to hear the music and be reminded.

Timmons stopped to eat some of his ice-cream cone. "I looked in the file, and in our rotation schedule this year's chaperoning duties fall on the science department. Since you're department chair I want you to be at the event and get commitments from three of the other teachers."

Caleb's jaw locked for a moment. "I can't."

"You must."

He shifted his weight. "I don't think you understand. I can't go to the Barn Dance."

"Special events are listed in the contract you signed when you took over as head of the department last year. I thought you knew that." Timmons's voice was gentle, but firm.

"Evidently I didn't read all the small print." Because he wouldn't have signed if he'd seen that.

"If you look, that's part of your role. I'll need you to lead the other volunteers next week as they brush up on the steps for square dancing, and you'll have to bring a partner to the dance so you can teach the students the steps involved."

"You're ordering me to bring a date?"

"Not ordering—more like, reminding you to fulfill your responsibility."

Caleb grabbed the bag of produce and headed to find

Shelby. Being surrounded by so many people had suddenly lost all its appeal. He needed home and time alone.

Most of all he needed to think of a reason not to attend the Barn Dance.

Maggie looped her arm through Paige's. "Have I told you how glad I am that you came to live with me?"

"Only about five or six times." Paige patted Maggie's hand as they walked down the sidewalk toward the center of town. Maggie said Goose Harbor held a farmer's market every Saturday and Paige had to be seen there if she wanted to successfully become a member of town.

"I still wish you'd let me pay something for rent."

"I couldn't."

Paige stumbled as her foot went off the edge of the sidewalk onto the grass. "I feel like a squatter sometimes—which is why, drumroll please, I'm meeting with a real-estate agent tomorrow after church to see some rental properties in town."

Maggie gave her arm a light squeeze. "You don't have to, you know that, right? I don't mind if you stay. It's nice having someone else in the private quarters with me."

"I need this—for me." Paige splayed her hand over her heart.

"I get that. Believe me. I do."

Paige waved to some of her students as they passed. "What about you, Maggie? I feel like you spend all your time serving others. What do you need to do, something just for you?"

Maggie laughed—a loud, carefree sound that ended with the smallest snort. "Get myself a man! But that's never going to happen."

"We don't need no men. Am I right?" Paige playfully elbowed Maggie in the ribs.

Maggie tugged on her arm, pulling Paige to a stop. "Can I say something?"

"Sure." Paige shrugged.

"Wishing for a man or a future marriage and family isn't a bad thing."

"No...but I don't think that a woman needs a man." Paige kept her voice low as people passed them on the sidewalk. Maggie sometimes had the oddest timing when it came to serious conversations.

"Right, but you make it seem like it's a bad thing to want that, or that a woman who wants that is being stupid or is wrong. It's not." Maggie clearly didn't feel the need to keep the conversation private or her voice low. "All I'm saying is just don't put too much stock in being alone. Okay?"

"Listen." The conversation needed to end. She'd just tossed the antiman card out there hoping for a laugh and a shared sisterhood wink. Old friends back home talked bad about the opposite gender all the time. What was Maggie's problem? "Wanting to be married is fine and all, but I think it's a stupid thing to hold your breath for."

"I have a feeling you didn't always believe that."

"Oh, really?"

"You were engaged once. Now you're so standoffish when the topic of men or dating comes up. I'm terrified that you've cut yourself off from the possibility of love."

Maggie had a motherly way about her, but Paige didn't need a mother right now; she just wanted a friend.

Maggie placed her hand on Paige's forearm. "What happened, Paige? You haven't told me yet."

Paige glanced behind her and brushed out of Maggie's touch. Okay, no one nearby right now. "You know what happened? Men lie, and I feel no need to be in a relationship just to find myself disappointed and hurt in the end."

Maggie crossed her arms. "Not all men."

A bitter laugh escaped her lips. "In my experience, it's all men."

"Sure, there's no such thing as a perfect human, so of course every relationship on this earth will disappoint you at some point. That's why I'm glad God's there and will never let us down."

God…there for her? He seemed to have better stuff to do.

So be it.

She'd gotten by this far without Him stepping in to help. Hadn't she?

It wasn't like she didn't want to be different. How many nights had she spent on her knees crying out for help? She wanted to trust Him—trust He was good like the people at her church in college said. Paige wanted it as badly as a drink of cool water in a desert wasteland, but she was afraid it was all a mirage and once again she'd be left flat on her face with nothing but a mouthful of sand to show for her efforts.

Maggie was still staring at her, waiting for a response.

"Oh. Of course." Paige needed to change the conversation.

A little old man with his pants pulled up past his belly button stepped out onto his porch and squinted into the sun. With a pronounced nose and a garland of gray wisps, he had to be close to her grandfather's age.

"There you are—the man of your dreams." Paige poked Maggie in the side. "Why don't you blow him a kiss?"

"Mr. Banks?" Maggie wrinkled her nose.

"Why not? It'll make his day." Paige winked.

"He's the town curmudgeon. He always claimed he was born on a Sunday and started doing chores that very Monday and that the rest of us should do the same." Maggie shook her head.

"Well, then, maybe he needs that kiss more than anyone," Paige joked.

"All right." Maggie shrugged. She let go of Paige's arm. "Morning, Mr. Banks."

"Eh?" The gruff grunt was Mr. Banks's formal greeting.

"This is for you." Touching her hand to her lips, Maggie kissed her palm and made like she was tossing it to the elderly man.

He reached out his hand and pretended to catch the kiss and hold it to his heart. "What a nice gesture. You just made this old man's day, girlie." Mr. Banks spoke louder than he needed to.

Maggie's cheeks turned red and she ducked her head. "You have yourself a good day."

"Guess he's not such a grump after all," Paige whispered, and they both started laughing. They approached the buildings that led to the center of town; all they needed to do now was make it to the corner and turn past the redbrick building to reach the square.

"You know," Paige continued, "you could marry him and maybe he'd leave you all his money." She chuckled.

Maggie didn't. She let go of Paige's arm.

Paige stopped and faced Maggie. "What did I say?"

"It's…" Maggie blinked rapidly. "It's nothing. Your turn." She pointed at a car pulling up the road. "You have to blow a kiss to whoever is in that car."

What if Principal Timmons drove that car? Paige bit her lip. But Maggie looked so upset all of a sudden, and maybe it would lighten the mood.

Paige nodded and kissed her hand. When the car came to a rest at the stop sign, she blew the kiss to a boy who looked about six years old sitting in the backseat. He scowled and stuck out his tongue as the car pulled away.

"Wow." Paige shook her head good-naturedly. "I had quite an effect on him."

Maggie doubled over in a fit of giggles. "Guess he likes girls about as much as you like boys."

Paige looked back at Maggie as she rounded the corner and subsequently smashed right into Caleb's solid chest.

"Careful, Paige." He grabbed her wrist to steady her. It felt all too familiar.

The bouquet he carried thumped to the ground. Who were those flowers for? Amy?

A pretty woman with wavy mocha hair peeked out from behind Caleb. "Is this her?"

He held Paige by the elbows and her hands rested on his biceps until, suddenly self-conscious, she pulled away.

Caleb and Paige both stooped to pick up the flowers, but instead banged heads.

"Ouch."

"Are you okay?"

"I'm fine." She rubbed her forehead. "Sorry about your flowers."

The girl with wavy hair stepped forward. "They're fine. They were just for the house anyway." She scooped the pretty blooms up and pressed them to her nose. Despite the warmth building that morning the girl wore a navy blue long-sleeved shirt and jeans. "Sandra's Boutique has the best lilies."

Caleb's hand was still on her arm. Paige stared at it. He slowly helped her stand and then let go. "This is my sister. Shelby." He jutted his finger to indicate the pixie-size woman next to him.

"I'm Paige." She extended her hand.

Shelby grinned at her. "You should know by now, we

don't really do the whole shake hands approach in this town." She reached over and gave Paige a hug. "Great to meet you." Shelby held on to Paige's upper arms and set her back to look at her face. "So you're the one who's been getting under my brother's skin? You're so beautiful. Caleb, why didn't you tell me how pretty she was?" She swatted her brother in the chest.

Caleb looked off to the left and acted like he couldn't hear Shelby, but Paige saw he was watching them.

"Caleb." Done laughing, Maggie finally joined them. "Why do you look like the dog that bit the porcupine?"

"Timmons wants me to chaperone the Barn Dance." Caleb worked his jaw back and forth.

Maggie tilted her head. "That'd be good for you."

"I think not."

Why? Paige swallowed questions she wanted to ask. The first line of defense for battling her attraction to Caleb would be to know the least about him that she could. Knowing made him personal, and each piece of information she learned made her more vulnerable to caring.

"Those two can waste time talking, but I say we go enjoy the market." Shelby looped her arm through Paige's. "Here, I'll show you around."

The town square around the corner was splashed in a downpour of sunlight. People milled in between rows of vendors set up in the grassy center of town. A couple of families sat together in the gazebo eating freshly made pastries. The small parking lot had been blocked off, and beyond that was the doughnut shop across the street with a mural that wrapped around the side of the building. The painting depicted children in every season—kids selecting Christmas trees, kids posing with pumpkins and kids running in a field of flowers with big, fat bumblebees dancing around them.

Paige was impressed at how much the vendors made the town square look like a country market. She'd driven past on her way back from Sarah's Home the other night, but it had just been a patch of grass and park benches then.

As they walked closer, the heady, sweet scent of ripe fruit and fresh-baked bread filled her lungs. Amber jars of honey caught the sunlight and cast prisms onto the ground. Tiny pumpkins decorated with painted faces in different expressions dotted every table. Pyramids of yellow corn, squash and zucchini filled a whole table, butting up against a refrigerated compartment on wheels with fresh meat and large blocks of orange cheese encased behind glass.

"Were you looking for anything in particular?" Shelby asked.

Paige glanced over her shoulder at where Caleb and Maggie talked on the corner. "Can I ask what you meant when you said I've been getting under Caleb's skin?"

Mayday! Why did she ask that? So much for telling herself not to find out more about him.

Shelby waved to a family near the red band shell. "Let's just say he brings you up—often."

Paige stopped. "In an I-can't-stand-that-girl way?"

The corners of Shelby's lips tipped up. "No. Not like that. But I think I've probably said too much already."

"Sorry." Paige ran her fingers along the edge of a table where a vendor sold bracelets. "I don't want you to break any sort of sisterly bond, but I guess I'm having a hard time understanding your brother."

Shelby turned and tilted her head. "Caleb's not hard to figure out. He's basically an open book. I mean, he takes care of everyone—way more than he needs to—loves kids and teaching, and keeps to himself for pretty much everything else."

"A regular Rochester." Paige selected two bracelets to try on.

"Huh?" Shelby wrinkled her nose.

"Sorry. English teacher." Paige laughed. "It's from the book *Jane Eyre*."

"Does this Rochester guy at least get a happy ending?"

"Eventually. But he's a grouch for almost half the book." Paige selected the orange cloth bracelet. She'd wear it to Sarah's Home this week and see if Smalls noticed.

"That sounds like my brother." Shelby rolled her eyes.

"What sounds like your brother?" Caleb's voice made both of the women jump.

His sister offered a silly grin. "Paige says you're like some fictional guy named Rochester."

Heat raced up Paige's neck. Hopefully Caleb didn't know English literature well enough to know who the character was. She spun around to meet his eyes.

He knew.

Caleb tilted his head and squinted at her. "That brooding guy with his wife locked in an attic?"

Shelby burst out laughing and fanned her face. "Oh. That's so funny. You didn't tell me that attic part." She sucked in air. "Have fun explaining that one." Shelby squeezed Paige's arm and turned to talk to the young family next to her.

Caleb bit back a smile. Paige always came off as so knowledgeable and put together, it was fun to catch her off her game.

Paige's cheeks turned candy-apple red. Her mouth fell open. She closed it. Then opened it again. "I guess I shouldn't have said that."

He shrugged and softened his voice. "I don't remember

that much about him. I haven't read that book since my high school days—and that was a long time ago."

She offered him a soft smile. "Hey. We're about the same age, so I'm going with it wasn't that long ago."

Turning back to the booth, she handed the orange bracelet and her credit card to the person manning the booth.

"Cash only." The clerk pointed to indicate a small handwritten sign on the table.

"Oh. I didn't bring any with me." Her cheeks flushed again. "Will you be here next week?"

Caleb pulled out his wallet and handed a few bills to the clerk. "I've got it."

Paige turned quickly toward him. She worked her lip between her teeth. "You don't have to."

The clerk handed him some change and the bracelet.

Caleb motioned for Paige to put out her wrist. "Perhaps I wanted to."

"I'll pay you back at school on Monday." She held out her arm.

His fingers brushed against her hand as he tied the bracelet on. "There's no need."

"I should." Her eyes darted to his.

He squeezed her hand awkwardly. "Consider it a welcome-to-town gift."

"Thank you." She spoke so softly he had to lean closer to hear her. She blinked a couple of times. It almost looked like she was holding back tears.

Over a bracelet? Perhaps it had been too long since someone offered her a gift for no reason other than they cared. Maybe she was low on money. Either way, he wouldn't push the issue.

They fell into step together.

She broke their silence first. "I picked orange because it made me think of Smalls."

Caleb chuckled. "That'll make his day when you tell him."

"He seems like a good guy." Paige glanced at a cart selling gelato.

"Smalls has a good heart." Caleb adjusted the bag of vegetables he carried. Ever since the first day at Sarah's Home, he'd wanted to find a way to warn Paige about getting close to the boy because of the family's connections. "But both of his older brothers are heavily involved in one of the gangs, so I worry about him a lot."

"Don't you see?" She stopped in her tracks and a small child darted around her. "That's why the work each of us do at Sarah's Home is so important."

Images of Smalls's brothers, Pete and Cameron, popped into his head. "We didn't save his older brothers."

"But you offered them another option."

"You really have a heart for the students there." He stared at her—the genuine hope in her voice and the shine in her eyes made him soften about Sarah's Home for the first time in a long time.

"I guess I believe everyone deserves equal opportunities."

He swallowed hard. "Which means you're still set on serving there in a long-term capacity?"

"Absolutely."

He let out a long breath. "I was afraid you'd say that."

"You're not getting rid of me. You know that, right?"

"I'd still like you to reconsider." And not because of any close ties to kids that might break her heart by disappointing her.

Paige stepped closer. "Just so you know—I did think about what you said the other day. I weighed the dangers, but I'm still going to be volunteering. Even if you don't like that."

"Can you at least promise me that you'll only go if I'm going to be there? I'd feel more comfortable about it if you'd agree to that." He put both his hands up to stop her from starting to talk. "Now, before you answer, let me tell you that I've only missed one night in the past two years."

She shrugged. "Doesn't sound like there's much to promise."

If he had his way, he wouldn't miss another day as long as Paige was going to be there. Sarah's Home needed him more than ever.

After Caleb left, Paige bought an ice-cream cone from Founder's Creamery and snagged a seat in the gazebo. She pulled up the email function on her phone and opened the note she'd received from Mom late last night. She hadn't thought they'd been serious about selling the place, but in less than a week her parents had found a buyer for her childhood home. When the sale happened, one more familiar thing would be gone from her life.

Paige rested her head in her free hand. Knowing her mother, she'd already started packing up the house, and Paige did not want Mom sifting through all her belongings. They were boxed in the garage at the moment, but when it came to her mother, anything was game. She made a note to talk to Maggie to find out if there was a place she could store her extra things if she went to get them.

Knowing she'd never spend another night under the roof of the home she grew up in stung a little bit. Then again, it also served as yet more confirmation that moving to Goose Harbor had been the right decision.

A couple of girls she knew as students congregated on the gazebo steps but didn't seem to notice her. They pointed at Amy, who happened to be strutting around the market in spandex pants and a sports bra, and started laughing.

"How much work do you think she's had done?" One girl snorted.

"Oh, tons. No one has a chest like that without surgery."

Amy now walked within earshot, but the girls weren't paying attention.

"She's such a joke. No one likes her."

"Please feel sorry for me…I'm stuck on the volleyball team with her."

"My dad said when she was in high school she slept with the whole football team and still no one asked her to prom."

"She's pathetic."

Why were girls so mean to each other? Paige's throat clammed up even though she wanted to tell them to stop.

Amy glanced over her shoulder at them and then made a beeline for the town hall. She swiped under her eyes before pushing through the front door. The sight finally spurred Paige to action.

She snapped to her feet and surged forward. "Girls, it's not okay to talk about someone like that."

They all froze—clearly unaware that she'd been sitting a few feet from them.

Finally one of them regained her composure. "She couldn't hear us."

They didn't get it.

"That doesn't matter. It's called respecting people and respecting other women. Being a girl in this world is difficult enough—we don't need to spend our time cutting each other down." Paige joined them on the steps. "Beyond that, she's a teacher at your school so she deserves your respect."

The shortest girl crossed her arms and jutted out her chin. "That doesn't mean we have to like her."

Paige sighed. "You're right to a point. We all click with some people and not with others and don't have control over that, but we do have control over our words and how we treat people. I want better for you girls than to use your words and conversations to hurt others or convince yourself you're better than someone."

They all mumbled that they understood, but who knew? She caught the short one rolling her eyes as they walked away. Paige was sure to end up in a Twitter status.

Collecting her bags, Paige made a split-second decision to check on Amy. If she had heard…

She crossed the street and opened the front door to the building. While the main portion of the town hall wasn't open on the weekends, the small lobby had access to restrooms and was left unlocked during the farmer's market. Paige walked into the women's restroom. Amy dabbed at her eyes in the farthest mirror. Clearly she'd been crying.

Paige approached her slowly. "Are you okay?"

Amy scowled at her. "You must have loved overhearing that. What a riot for you."

"Actually, I hated it." Paige balanced her purse and bag on the sink. "No one should talk about another person like that."

Amy faced her. "What if what they said was true? What if I've done every single thing they said?" Her face crumpled. "No wonder people hate me."

Paige debated moving closer to hug her, but Amy wouldn't have received that well.

Help me say the right thing.

Paige ducked into a stall and collected a long strip of toilet paper. She handed it to Amy. "If what they said was true, all that stuff happened in the past. If you don't want those things to be true, you don't have to be that person tomorrow. That's the best thing about each day—it's the chance for a do-over in life."

"But that stuff doesn't go away."

"Sure. It'll always be a part of your makeup. It all adds to your story and shapes who you become, but it doesn't have to be who you are. Does that make sense?" Paige offered what she hoped was an encouraging smile.

"Maybe."

"Can I do anything for you?"

Amy turned her back on Paige. She yanked a hooded sweatshirt from her bag and tugged it on over her sports bra. "Don't tell anyone about this."

"Of course not."

Amy wanted to be left alone, so Paige gathered her bags and made the trek back to the West Oaks Inn. The whole walk home Paige thought about her conversation with Amy. The woman had so much in her past that held her back. Amy could have been a well-liked person if she would let go of the baggage and drop the prickly exterior in order to open herself up to others.

She paused on the bridge and traced her fingers over the petals in the latest bouquet Ida had left for her dead husband. Ida dwelled on yesterday too, but she didn't let it tarnish her warm persona.

What in Paige's life did she need to leave in the past in order to move forward and be different tomorrow?

Distrust, disappointment and hurt.

The words winged their way across her heart. Despite what it looked like, no one had the perfect life—not Maggie, not Amy, not Ida, not Caleb, and she'd only just met her, but probably not Shelby, either. Yet they seemed able to open themselves up to people and trust others.

Perhaps Paige could do the same.

Chapter Eight

Paige slung the heavy messenger bag over her shoulder and headed into Sarah's Home. After three weeks of working with the students and seeing their potential, tonight she was excited to share her plan to help them go to college. When she pushed through the front door, Smalls and two more of the students were there to greet her.

"You came back." Smalls grinned.

She nodded as her eyes adjusted to the dimmer light inside the building. "You always sound so surprised." Paige motioned for the three students to follow her into the side room where there were tables that could accommodate all of them. Thankfully, these were the three students she had decided to hunt down tonight to talk to because they were seniors in high school or, like Smalls, had graduated already.

"That's because each time you leave I always think that's the last time we'll see you. No disrespect, but a pretty woman like you just don't belong on this side of Brookside. People like you don't stick around in places like this. You're too good for it."

Her heart twisted in a knot. *People like you.* Who had told the teen such a thing?

Praying for the right words, Paige set her bag on the table and then looked up, making sure she had the attention of all three of the students. "That's not true." She paused to make eye contact with each of them. "There is no such thing as *people like me,* okay? There are just people, and we all have value. Not one person is better or worth more than another."

She pulled the stack of pamphlets and college booklets out of her bag. "At the school where I work, we have a whole wall of information about colleges, and I noticed that there was nothing available like that here so I brought some with me tonight." She fanned the booklets full of flashy photos of college students smiling in dorm rooms and chatting on manicured lawns across the table.

Smalls crossed his arms and leaned back in his chair. "That's because none of us go to college. We can't even get out of this city. No one here's got the money for that."

The girl seated next to Smalls leafed through a catalog for one of the state universities. "Let's be straight, Miss W. We barely make it out of high school."

Paige pursed her lips for a minute. She wanted to scream. Who had taught these students that education was out of their reach? Who told them they were stuck without hope?

Give them hope.

She took a deep breath. "I believe that each of you is capable of going on to college because I think every single one of you has ideas that can change the world."

Smalls pushed back in his seat and narrowed his eyes at the stack of catalogs. "A body doesn't have to go to school to change the world."

"You're right." Paige nodded. "Completely right. But if you wanted to go to college, I wanted you to know that it's a very real option."

"Belief doesn't pay the bills." The girl wistfully sighed and placed the college handout back on top of the stack.

"No, it doesn't." Paige pulled another bundle of paperwork out from her bag. "But scholarships and grants, along with work-study programs, can help. Right here in my hands I'm holding the information for more than thirty scholarships that you could each be eligible for. I spent last weekend researching each of them, and I really think any of you have a good chance."

She handed a packet for a small college nearby that awarded money to people wishing to pursue creative writing and performance to Smalls. With his love of slam poetry, he'd be a shoo-in for the university's program.

Smalls scanned the paper. "You did all this...for us?"

"It wasn't much."

He raised his eyebrows. "Looks like an awful lot."

"If anyone is interested, I'm happy to help you with entrance essays and the paperwork for the scholarships. I'll walk with you through each step if you want." She squeezed the hand of the student who'd stayed silent. "I'll even drive you to college visits if you decide you're considering one of them."

"Thank you." The girl next to Smalls breathed the words more than said them.

Caleb stood in the doorway listening to Paige talk to the seniors about going to college. He'd never thought about taking them through the college-application process, let alone arranging college visits. But that was because these teens didn't want to go to college. Besides, even if they wanted to, most of their grades wouldn't garner them acceptance to a lot of places.

He cleared his throat. "Marty's serving up root-beer floats in the kitchen and says he's going to start his talk on managing money in about five minutes. You guys might want to head in there before everything's gone."

"What money are we supposed to be managing?" Smalls laughed. He tapped on Caleb's bicep on his way into the hall. "Unless you let me manage your money— I'd only take a little off the top."

"That's what I'm afraid of." Caleb grinned at him. The two other students filed out of the room, each with some of Paige's college paperwork under their arms.

Paige left her bag on the table and moved to follow the students, but Caleb caught her arm before she could leave. "Can we talk for a minute?"

"Sure." The word might have been casual, but the tilt of her head was not.

"Listen. I think it's great that you believe in the kids and want to give them some hope." Caleb tried to think of the correct words.

"But." Paige crossed her arms and raised her chin. "It sounds like you're about to say that I shouldn't believe in them."

He took a step closer and lowered his voice. "But maybe encouraging them to try the impossible isn't the best thing."

"The impossible?" Her voice went higher.

"The reality is that most of these kids aren't cut out for college."

"One, they aren't kids. They're young adults who are about to be considered independents in the world, and we need to prepare them for that." She uncrossed her arms, her hands landing on her hips. "And two, what's the point of having a place like Sarah's Home if the person running the show doesn't believe in the students here?"

The conversation was getting out of hand quickly.

Caleb motioned frantically with his palms toward the ground. "Keep your voice down."

"Why?" Paige took a step closer. Her hands were fisted at her sides now, her arms shaking. "Are you afraid they'll find out that their leader doesn't even believe in them enough to offer a chance to get out of this city? I'm really glad the board calls the shots and not you."

He closed the door to muffle their voices. Hopefully no one down the hall had heard her. When he turned back around, she raised her eyebrows and tapped her foot. If they weren't in the middle of a debate, the sight would have made him smile. She was too small to ever look intimidating.

She wasn't understanding. He believed in these students. Didn't he? Of course he did. But he also knew their situations and realities.

Caleb took a deep breath. "The fact of the matter is that some of them will never get out of this city. That's just how life here is. Sarah's Home exists to teach them to thrive here and show them that it's possible to live in Brookside without turning to crime."

"But—"

He straightened his spine. "Telling them that they can achieve whatever their heart's desire is only setting them up to fail. Is that the best? Letting them face even more disappointments and discouragement than they've all already had to live through?"

Paige grabbed the door handle. "They deserve the chance to try if they want to. I'm not saying college is a fix-all for all their problems, or even that it's for all of them. But every single one of them should know that if that's what they want then all of us here will do whatever it takes to help them because we believe in them and want the best for them. Period. And if that's not the case, then

Sarah's Home should close its doors tonight and never open again."

She yanked open the door and fast-walked down the hall.

Caleb sank into a nearby chair and rested his head in his hands. He replayed the conversation and cringed at his own words. Paige was right. He'd stopped believing in the students here. Sarah's Home had become an obligation—a task to complete to honor Sarah—no longer a place he rushed to because he cared about the individual students. When had that shift happened? Where had his joy in serving gone?

He glanced around the room, his gaze landing on the pile of college catalogs. As much as he didn't want to admit it, having Paige around was the best thing for Sarah's Home. For the students. For him. She was changing his heart more than he cared to acknowledge at the moment. Paige cared about these teens and their future. Really cared.

Now Caleb wanted to care again, too.

"Who knew finding a place to rent would be that easy?" Maggie dried off the glass mason jars she had the inn guests use for drinking lemonade on the porch. "Usually the rentals are hard to come by because even though they free up some in the off-season, tourists still rent them for weekend use year-round."

Paige scanned her phone and searched for the closest place she could rent a small truck. Before her courage waned, she needed to get on the road to Chicago, face her parents and their questions again and collect the rest of her stuff.

She glanced back at Maggie. "It looks like a storybook house. A couple lilac bushes line the house and the Realtor said the entire front patch will bloom with tulips in the spring. The house is sky-blue, all except for the entrance. It's built of a bunch of stones that form a circular area by the front door. Almost like a castle turret, even if it's only one story."

"I think I know the house." Maggie finished tucking the jars away in the cabinet. "The third one on Belmont Lane?"

Paige nodded. "It's only a one bedroom, but that's all I need. If I leave for Chicago in the next hour I'll be able to get there, pack the rest of my stuff into the truck and be back here before dinner tonight."

"How long is the drive?"

"Just over two hours." Paige fished through the contents of her purse. Lip gloss, gum, wallet—all the essentials for her spontaneous day trip were accounted for.

"You must be one quick packer."

"Oh, no. My stuff's all boxed up already." Seeing as she had thought she'd be moving it into Bryan's condo at any moment, the boxes had stayed in Mom and Dad's garage. Waiting. Now they could be liberated. Besides, it would be nice not to have her stuff divided between two homes.

The lease she'd signed didn't start for another month, but she couldn't stand one more day of wondering if her mom had rummaged through her things or tossed any of her belongings. Always a minimalist, her mom didn't seem to grasp the concept of having a sentimental attachment to some of her things. Once Maggie offered her the use of the basement to store her boxes, she knew she needed to get back to Chicago right away.

Paige clicked the GPS function on her phone. "Is there an easier way to get to Smithton's Rent-All?"

"Ugh. Don't go to Smithton's." Maggie pulled a face.

"What's wrong with them?" Paige set down her phone.

"Someone need a truck?" Caleb's voice made Paige jump.

She whirled around. "How do you always sneak up on me?"

"The way I see it, you're the one always running into me." Caleb grinned and snagged a carrot stick off the platter Maggie was about to set out in the lobby.

"Oh! You." Maggie swatted at his hand, a smile showing she didn't really care. She picked up the platter and used her hip to open the door that led to the guest area of the inn.

Picking her phone up again, Paige tried to ignore Caleb. She needed to figure out a plan to get her boxes, and talking with him right now wouldn't help that. Besides, she was still frustrated about his attitude toward the students at Sarah's Home after their disagreement the other day.

She scrolled through the list of truck-rental places. Why did so many of them close by noon on Saturday? Saturday was when people moved. In the Chicago area the businesses were open extra late on the weekends. So finally, a downside to small town living.

Caleb braced his hands on the island. "Paige, I need to talk—"

She held up her hand. "I'm kind of in a hurry right now."

His face fell. "Oh."

"I'm sorry." She put the phone back into her pocket. "I need to get to one of the truck-rental places before they close."

"How about the use of a free one?"

Paige adjusted the hair ties on her wrist before looping her purse on her shoulder. "I'd say that's even better."

"Where do you need to go?"

"Chicago."

He crossed his arms over his chest. "Is it just for the day?"

She nodded. "My parents are moving, so I want to pick up the rest of my belongings and come back here tonight."

Caleb pulled out his car keys. "I'll drive you, but I want to talk first."

"I've found that when someone says that, it usually isn't a good thing." Paige perched on the edge of the stool.

"The other day at Sarah's Home—"

"Please." She looked down at her fingers. "I don't want to fight again. Not if we're going to spend the day together."

"Hear me out." He pulled out the stool beside her and sat down. His knee bumped against hers. "I stopped by today hoping to see you. I thought a lot about what you said—about our need to believe in the students. And you're right. I…I'd lost sight of that, and I wanted to thank you for reminding me."

She glanced up at him and was met by his soft chocolate gaze. "Really?"

"When I lost Sarah…I realized I've been holding on to a lot of anger and directed it at Sarah's Home and inadvertently onto the students there. We never found out who attacked her that night, and I've always wondered if one of the students knew and didn't say anything. I think—" His voice failed him for a moment. "I think I stopped caring about them for a while because of it."

Paige fought the urge to take his hand. Her heart twisted for all he'd been through and had to process—was still processing two years after his wife's death. "Caleb. That's all understandable."

"I'm sorry for how I acted the other day. Well, not just that time. I'm sorry for how I've acted each time we've been to Sarah's Home. You keep working so hard with those students, and I've been such a roadblock. I do care about them. I wouldn't have kept the place open if I didn't."

"It makes sense, though."

He still seemed to be waiting for something more.

So she added, "I forgive you."

Caleb let out a long breath. "Since it looks like we're going to be around each other a lot, can you do me a favor? If I start to do it again, I'm giving you permission to pull me aside and point that out."

Trying to lighten the mood, she smiled. "Noted." She fiddled with the strap of her purse. "Was that everything?"

"Yes." He jingled his keys. "Are we leaving now?"

"If you're sure that's fine."

His eyebrows knit together and he stared at her. "I wouldn't have offered if it wasn't."

Within ten minutes they were both buckled in the truck and pulling out onto the interstate. She stacked the five reading books he had lying on the bench in a plastic bag she found in his glove box to keep them from sliding all over the place. *Watership Down, Lord of the Flies, The Rough Riders, Undaunted Courage* and *The Great Gatsby*—all library books. Such a diverse reading list. Who was this man? She bit back all the questions she wanted to ask. Questions and conversation about books would only serve to paint a more charming image of him in her mind than already existed.

Things needed to stay surface level and friendly. No feelings. If she was going to build a life in Goose Harbor, keeping things platonic with Caleb was a must. Getting attached to a man meant pain—always—and she'd seen plenty of that to last her quite a while.

Chapter Nine

Caleb glanced at Paige as he turned into a gated residential community. He'd never actually been to the area, so when Paige had told him she lived in Chicago, he'd pictured a row of small brick bungalow homes situated close enough to reach out a window and touch the neighbor's siding. Alleys that weren't well plowed in winter, that sort of city living. She'd failed to mention that her parents lived in the wealthy section of the suburbs.

Behemoth homes, bigger than two of Maggie's old Victorian inns put together, loomed on either side of the quiet street. People had their own tennis courts and private, fenced-in basketball courts in their backyards. Garages here housed four cars.

Caleb rubbed the grease stain on his jeans. Why hadn't he changed before they left? What sort of impression would beat-up work boots, a rolled-up flannel shirt and stained jeans make on the Windoms? Maybe he should stay in the truck when they got there. Although, that would mean her lifting all the boxes herself, which he'd never let happen.

"Turn down Lavender Avenue and it's the second house on the left," Paige directed him.

The Windoms' home fit in perfectly with the neighborhood. The white house boasted four two-story pillars, and he guessed it had room for six or more bedrooms upstairs. A large sculpture in the middle of a fountain in the front yard spewed water. People had stuff like that in their yards?

The tires of his truck had no more than hit the curb when an older woman and a younger man stepped out the front door and started walking toward them.

The man stopped before continuing down the driveway. He pulled his phone from his back pocket, turned his back to them and talked to someone.

Paige stiffened. One of her hands locked around the edge of her seat, the other around the strap of her purse. "Why is he here? I can't do this."

Caleb's senses went on alert. He popped the truck into Park and then reached over and placed his hand on top of hers. "What's wrong?"

"Him." Her lip trembled and she started that rapid-fire blink thing he remembered from the first time they met.

Realization surged through his heart. "Does he have something to do with the wedding dress?"

Paige nodded once, sharply.

"Do you want me to tell him to go?"

She gently tugged her hand out from under his and drew in a long breath. "No one tells Bryan to leave. It doesn't work like that."

All the glow that normally filled her features drained from her face.

"Could you start loading the boxes? They're stacked in the garage." She pointed to the last open door. "I'd like to get out of here as fast as possible."

He nodded and climbed out of the truck. What else

could he do? Paige needed someone to stand beside her to help fight her dragons, but evidently, she didn't want that man to be him.

Willing her hands to stop shaking, she slipped out of the truck. What she'd mistaken early on in her relationship with Bryan for a butterflies-in-the-stomach feeling had really always been a bubbling terror in her gut. Around him, she'd never been free to talk or state any opinion. And yet she'd stayed because her mind had been tricked into believing that he was right to tread on her plans and desires. Bryan had always gotten his way, and she could no longer blame him for that.

She hadn't possessed the courage or ability to speak up for herself.

Away from Bryan for the past few months, she'd been able to start healing. But was it enough? The sick feeling racing up her throat said no.

Mom marched forward, dressed in her normal heels and pearls. "Who is that man you came with?"

Hi would have been nice. Hearing she'd been missed would have been better.

"A friend."

Her mom's jaw went slack. "You're now accustomed to befriending lumberjacks? I thought I raised you better than that." Her whisper was no doubt loud enough for Caleb to hear from where he loaded boxes.

Heat rushed up the back of Paige's neck. "Mom, that's rude."

Mom popped her hands on her hips. "So is not greeting my guest." She smiled sweetly at Bryan.

"Why did you invite him here when you knew I'd be stopping by today?" She shouldn't have given her mom warning that she was coming. The scolding of showing up unannounced would have been better than dealing with Bryan.

Like a giddy schoolgirl, Mom's eyes went big and she clamped onto Paige's wrist. "He wants to give you back the ring, sweetheart. The ring! Do you know what that means?" She started to drag Paige toward Bryan. "Well, I'll just leave you two alone. Don't be foolish, Paige." Mom winked at Bryan and strolled back into the house.

Paige commanded her heart to stop racing and her mind to work fast enough to be able to handle standing up to Bryan.

"Hey, babe." Bryan leaned in to hug her and Paige side-stepped him.

"Don't 'hey, babe' me. Why are you here?" Pretty good. Better than she'd ever done at standing up to him before. If only she could keep the quiver out of her voice.

He blinked a couple of times in mock disbelief. With his blond hair styled with copious amounts of gel, his bleached white teeth and designer polo that probably cost more than Caleb's truck was currently worth, Paige wondered what she ever saw in Bryan. Besides the facts that his father served in the Senate, he could offer her a life-style she'd grown used to and dating him made her mom happy—nothing. At least, nothing that meant anything to her. Not anymore.

How quickly what ranked as essential to her had changed. After a couple of weeks in Goose Harbor, she never again wanted to live in the affluent manner she'd been raised in. The people in her new town had small homes that held just what they needed, but more significantly, their lives were marked by strong friendships and a willingness to help their neighbors. Those things were important to her, too, now.

Bryan stepped closer, into her personal space. He

placed his hands on her arms where her sleeves ended and rubbed his thumbs against her skin. "Don't be like that. I've missed you."

"I don't want to do this. Leave me alone." She stepped out of his hold, yanked a ponytail holder off her arm and piled her hair into a bun.

"Tsk. Tsk." Bryan grabbed her wrist. Hard. "Who tells their fiancé to leave them alone?"

"You're not my fiancé." She tried to pull away.

"Listen." He jerked her so his mouth was right by her ear. "Everyone thinks you're a fool. They feel sorry for you, really—the girl who can't commit to a good guy."

"You cheated—"

His fingers dug into her skin. "Did you really think I'd let you make me look bad? You don't get to call off our wedding, Paige. But don't worry. It works out well. Everyone thinks better of me now. All our friends think I'm the height of understanding because I told them the wedding has been postponed while I allow you to go find yourself in Michigan. But soon enough, your time there will be over. Do you hear me?"

She braced her hands on his chest and applied pressure. "Why would you even still want me to marry you? We don't love each other."

Instead of getting the hint and letting go, he latched onto her other wrist and smiled down at her like the Cheshire cat. "You have the right upbringing and family to be the perfect wife for when I run for office. We'll be a good fit, you'll see."

"I'll never marry you." She shoved hard enough to finally get out of his hold and whirled around. Caleb stood near his truck, brow low, watching them.

On her heels, Bryan stalked down the grass and hopped into his BMW. Why hadn't she noticed the scorching red car right away when they pulled down the street? He must have slammed on the gas because the BMW flew down Lavender Avenue in two seconds flat.

Caleb forced himself to stay rooted in the spot next to the truck. His heart pounded like a war drum, and it wasn't from the effort of loading all the boxes as fast as he could. He watched the exchange between Paige and the golden boy and had ground his molars with not saying something. She'd done the thing with her hair that he noticed before—pulling it up when she felt uncomfortable. On one hand, it was good to know he'd read her mannerism right; on the other, his gut churned thinking of the number of times she'd done the same thing when he talked to her.

Did conversation with him make Paige feel small and insignificant like she appeared to feel when talking to Golden Boy? She'd visibly shrunk while that man loomed over her. If he had held on to Paige for thirty more seconds, then Caleb would have stormed over. He would have earlier if he'd known the situation better—if he'd known whether Paige would receive that sort of help well.

Paige offered a weak smile to him as she walked, slow and almost wobbly, down the driveway. "Thanks for loading the boxes. I should have helped."

He looped his thumbs on his pants pockets. "Are you okay? 'Cause you don't look like you're okay."

Paige pursed her lips together and shook her head. Tears started to run down her face. She swiped at them with her palm.

Caleb felt helpless. She looked so defenseless. A deep longing to protect her rose up in his chest. He decided then that moving forward he would stand between her and whatever danger was out there. Golden Boy couldn't treat her poorly any longer. Caleb would go out of his way to make her feel safe and cherished.

Cherished? Where had that come from?

He didn't know her well enough, did he?

Paige toed the ground. "I walk away from every conversation with him feeling like I'm not worth anything," she whispered.

"He's wrong." It came out as a fierce growl. Caleb closed the space between them in two steps and gathered her to his chest. To his surprise, she unlaced her arms and drew them around his back, pressing her head into his shoulder.

His hand covered her silky hair as he pressed his cheek against the side of her head. "That's his sin. His problem. Do you hear me, Paige? You had worth beyond measure from the moment God created you, and no one can take that away. Not that man. And not your feelings."

They stood together for a couple of minutes before Paige pushed lightly out of his hold. She went into the house to say goodbye to her parents and then they left for Goose Harbor. Paige spent the ride home silently gazing out the window, and Caleb spent the ride home fighting the urge to reach over and take her hand.

He couldn't pinpoint it, but slowly—like the changing of seasons—Paige had tiptoed into his heart. The realization made panic surge through his veins.

After seeing her ex-fiancé tower over her like a bridge troll, Caleb never wanted to let Paige get hurt again. But Paige wasn't easily convinced to be careful like Sarah had been. Paige would keep taking risks. Paige would keep going to Brookside and keep forging relationships with the urban youth.

And Caleb would now do everything in his power to protect her.

* * *

Paige's thoughts on the way back from Chicago became one huge mud puddle. Her mom would be disappointed with how she treated Bryan. Then again, she couldn't make choices in her life based on whether or not they pleased her mother. Not anymore.

Bryan accused her of being a fool. *The girl who can't commit to a good guy.*

Was there something wrong with her—some reason why her relationships never seemed to work out?

Caleb switched off the music. "I know you've had a long day, so if you want to be done, just say so, but I was wondering if you want to swing by the dunes before heading to Maggie's?"

She pictured the calm lake rolling in steadily and the relaxing feel of sand between her toes. Caleb would be with her, of course. But that didn't bother her. If one thing could be said for the man, it was that he was great at comforting confused women.

"Let's go. That might be just the stress relief I need."

Caleb turned into the Dunes State Park and they climbed out of the truck. Paige stretched; it felt good to move her legs after sitting for so long. They picked a spot at the top of the largest dune and dropped down in the sand, side by side. She tugged off her socks and shoes, enjoying the feel of the warm sand against her feet.

If she squinted, she could make out boats on the horizon of Lake Michigan. Probably fishermen, or the tour boat that went into the lake for a dinner cruise and a sunset-viewing party each evening.

The past few weeks in Goose Harbor became a jumble in her mind. Caleb arguing with her about Sarah's Home and his lighthearted sister, Shelby. Maggie with flour in her hair and Ida reminding her again and again and again to leave room for love. The heartbreaking stories of each of the students involved with Sarah's Home and the odd war Amy seemed to be fighting against Paige.

She'd coached Amy to let go of the past in order to move forward. It would make Paige a hypocrite if she didn't at least consider what she needed to let go of in order to become a better person in the future.

Had she forgiven Bryan for cheating on her? If not, would forgiving him mean—like Mom had said—that she should take him back?

Her stomach roiled. She couldn't. Wouldn't. She'd rather stay cut off from others than deal with Bryan's constant desire to make all her decisions for her. Being with him could never be considered actually living.

Okay. So…perhaps forgiving men from her past simply meant that she couldn't hold other men responsible for the mistakes they had made.

That would be difficult. So difficult.

How would she ever know when a man was trustworthy enough? The men in her past had all tricked her, at least for a while. Some longer than others. Who was to say she wouldn't fall for a man like that again even if she tried not to?

She curled her hands into the sand and let the grains filter through her fingers.

Letting go of that hurt would mean opening herself to the possibility of another man who would be able to hurt her again. But if she wanted to move forward, that was her only option.

Caleb shifted in the sand next to her, breaking Paige from her thoughts.

Resting his elbows on his knees, he studied her, not the water or the beach. "What are you thinking about?"

"Just…everything." Paige made eye contact. Those eyes would get her every time.

Could she trust a friendship with Caleb? She'd had more contact with him recently than with any other man. What if he let her down and she ended up hurt? What if he was nothing better than a cheater, as well?

Worse, what if she started to feel something for him?

Less than a foot of space between them, they sat together for another couple of minutes.

Caleb broke the silence first. "That first day I met you… You don't have to tell me if you don't want to, but I've wondered."

With her gaze locked on the water, she weighed telling him. But if she was going to try to trust men, then she should start by being honest herself. "I broke off my engagement." She adjusted how she sat and her knee brushed Caleb's. He didn't move.

Paige swallowed and continued. "I thought Bryan was *the one*. I'd had a couple boyfriends before him that just… didn't care."

"Didn't care?" Caleb's voice went up, as if what she said was the hardest thing to believe.

Might as well tell him everything. She sucked in a deep breath. "In high school, I had a boyfriend named Jay. He was the pastor's son at the church I grew up in. After a month of dating he told me he thought God had brought us together and that we'd be together forever. That was a week before he went on a mission trip to South Africa without me since my parents wouldn't let me go." Paige found a small twig under the sand and chucked it down the dune. "Yeah, he came back, and suddenly God had told him that Stacy, a girl he met on the trip, was really the one for him and not me."

She rolled her eyes. "They're married now and have four kids. So, I guess Jay was right about that."

Caleb leaned back a bit, his arms bracing his weight and hands in the sand. His fingers touched hers. "I'm sorry that happened to you."

"It was high school. I'm over it." She shrugged. "Then there was Tommy in college. We dated for two and a half years. Tommy took me ring shopping to find out what I liked, and then a month later Tommy dumped me for my roommate."

"Ouch." Caleb's hand covered hers now. She didn't move it.

"After that, I told myself I wouldn't get into a relationship until I could know for certain that the guy loved me and that I knew him well enough to believe he wouldn't leave me right away."

Caleb sat up and turned to face her. As he did, he laced his fingers with hers and cupped his other hand around their entwined ones. She couldn't tell if it was a gesture of comfort that he would do to anyone, if he felt badly for her, or wanted to prove that men didn't find her repulsive. Whatever the reason, the touch of another person felt good. Maybe too good. But she'd worry about that later.

"About four years after graduation I ran into Bryan, who I've known my whole life. We grew up in the same neighborhood but hung out with different people in school. When he asked me out, I didn't say yes right away because I wanted to be sure."

Caleb offered her hand a squeeze.

"Bryan kept pursuing me. Unlike Tommy and Jay, it felt like he actually cared and wanted to be involved in every aspect of my life. It was only after we broke up that I realized how controlling he was. He separated me from all my friends, all my hobbies, and convinced me to put in my resignation at school since he didn't want his wife to have a job. Anyway, we were engaged within six months, and I thought I finally had my happily ever after.

"He was already living in our condo, but I wanted to stay with my parents until the wedding. He pressured me to come live with him before we were married and that's the only thing I stuck to my guns about, which probably cost me the relationship in the end."

That's not true. Bryan should have waited.

The thought came out of nowhere and made her pause.

"He worked long hours in his firm downtown, so I decided to surprise him with dinner one night. I went to the condo and saw his car and just figured he'd gone in and taken a nap after work. Instead, I found him tangled up with another woman in our bed." She shook her head, trying to shove the image out of her mind. "I tossed the ring at his head and left. Oh, and my mom tried to convince me to stay with Bryan—she still wants me to go back to him."

"But he cheated on you."

"She said he did what all men do and to get over it."

"That's not true."

"I told her the same thing, and she popped that bubble real quick. She told me my dad's cheated on her with seven different women in the span of their marriage. My dad... I used to look up to him so much."

Caleb brushed his thumb on her cheek, catching tears she hadn't realized she was crying. Then he tugged the hand he held and pulled her in for a hug. She welcomed the contact, releasing his hand and drawing her arms around his back.

"That should have never happened," Caleb whispered into her hair. "You are worth cherishing. You are worth being faithful to. You are worth the truth."

The words were like a benediction working into all her broken memories.

You are worth the truth.

Chapter Ten

Caleb held Paige until she lightly pushed back from him. Without knowing how she'd react, he placed his hands on either side of her face to frame it. His thumbs brushed right below her eyes, which shone with tears she kept back. He examined the constellations of freckles across her nose and cheek and her pursed lips.

"Did you hear what I said? You have worth, and any man would be crazy not to notice that," he whispered.

Paige nodded and blinked a bunch of times.

Everything inside told him to lean in and kiss her. He moistened his lips, but he couldn't. Paige had been used, left and disappointed by men three times now. Make that four counting her father. What could Caleb offer her? A whole lot more hurt. That was what.

Even though he'd been married for a couple of years, he knew so little about women. He knew plenty about Sarah—but not women in general.

With Sarah he'd known when to lean in, what each of her expressions meant and what she needed without her asking. Being with Sarah had been second nature since he'd known her his whole life. He never once had to ask Sarah out for a date. They both just knew they'd do something together on Friday night after school. His marriage proposal consisted of taking her to pick out a ring and putting it on her finger the next weekend.

How could he be certain that if he started something with Paige he'd be able to carry through with his promises? Sure, he believed he could, but he'd thought the same with Sarah. In the end he hadn't been able to take care of her. Not really. Had he ever actually asked Sarah what she needed? Or just assumed like Bryan had with Paige?

He swallowed hard.

Thoughts seared his conscience and made his stomach uneasy. He needed to get up and move. Caleb dropped his hands away from Paige's face. "Come for a walk with me." He offered his hand to help her up.

She squinted at him, her head tilted. "I should probably put my shoes back on."

He had to start walking. Movement was the only way to still his guilt about the mistakes he made in his marriage. "We'll come back and get them later. It's just sand. You'll be fine."

"Okay." She slipped her hand into his.

They stumbled down the steep edge of the sand dune that led to the lakeshore, making sure to avoid the sections where tall grasses grew since Paige walked barefoot. A slight breeze whisked coolness off the water and wrapped around them. The evening would get cold quickly.

Caleb scooped up three round rocks and tried to skip them across the water. Each landed with a plunk.

Paige stood six feet away to his left. Her arms crossed, watching him.

He dusted the sand from his hands and motioned for her to walk along the edge that would soon be covered by water. "Thank you for telling me all that stuff. I know that can't be easy."

She shrugged. "It was time to tell someone."

Up the beach, a flock of Canada geese hunkered near a patch of dune grass.

"Watch where you step." He pointed at the geese.

Paige ran her palms back and forth over her cheeks and then laughed for the first time. "The college I went to had geese everywhere. Sometimes you couldn't walk to class without ruining your shoes. We used to joke that they should let some hunters come onto the property and take care of them."

"Do you know it's illegal to kill that breed of goose?"

The wind picked up, bringing a chill in off the water's surface. He'd have to keep the walk short since Paige didn't have a coat on.

"Seriously?" Paige's mouth fell open.

"Federal offense."

She fanned her arm out to indicate the flock like a tour guide at a museum. "There are so many of them."

Caleb grinned at her shock. He rested his foot on a piece of driftwood. "That's because they're the most successful comeback story. Nationwide they were hunted to the point where they were put on the endangered species list. The scientists trying to help save them searched, but after a few years of not finding any geese, they were moved to the extinct list."

"You're kidding me. Those things are like rats."

He smiled and shook his head. "Finally someone found one flock of geese on a small pond in Minnesota. Only about ten to fifteen of them left in the world. They used that flock to repopulate the species." He pointed to the flock on the beach. "You can see how successful the scientists were."

"I had no idea." She turned and shook her head at the geese. "I don't think I'll look at them the same again."

Caleb broke a branch off the driftwood log and turned the weathered wood over and over in his hand. "That's what I love about teaching science. I've always found it has the power to teach truth in such tangible ways."

"Really now?" She grinned and popped her hands onto her hips. "And what sort of truth does a story about a bunch of geese teach?"

He tossed the stick into the lake. "Even when you feel like something about your life or your world has been destroyed, even when other people have hunted and harmed your heart to near extinction, even when you get to the point where you want to go hide on some obscure lake where you can't be found, you can think about the geese. If they'd stayed there without being found then they'd be gone."

He finally faced Paige and made eye contact. He hadn't realized that he'd taken a couple of steps away from her as he spoke. "You and I aren't that different from them, are we? We can stay on that pond or we can be repaired. Except unlike them, the choice is ours."

"See, that's the hard part. If someone could just— oww!" Paige crumpled in the sand.

Caleb dropped to her side. "What happened? What's wrong?"

"Ouch. Ouch. Ouch. Man. That *really* hurt." Cradling her foot, Paige rocked back and forth.

"Let me see." He grabbed her ankle to get her to stop moving. Blood dripped between her fingers where she held her foot. Because of the blood, he couldn't make out how deep the cut was. It only took a second to locate the perpetrator, a broken bottle concealed under a thin layer of sand.

Old fears rose up to haunt him. The same words he'd fought when Shelby got burned and Sarah died. *Your*

*fault. You told her it would be okay. You should have pro-
tected her.*

Could he deny those inner taunts? Not this time.

The burn of pain lanced up Paige's leg.

A moment ago she'd been strolling on the beach, enjoying the feel of the wet sand under her steps. Without
warning it had suddenly felt like twenty bees stinging the
bottom of her foot at once. What happened?

Shuddering, she instinctively touched the gash. A chill
coursed through her body as her bangs fell in front of her
eyes. The very center of her foot felt like it was being
feasted on by fire ants. Something wet and warm seeped
through her fingers.

She blinked back gathering tears and tried to focus on
Caleb. "Can you make it stop?"

"I'm going to pick you up." He drew one arm behind her
back and the other under her knees. "Put your arm around
my neck, okay? I'm going to take you to the immediate-
care clinic in town."

With a few seconds to let the shock wear off, Paige
worked her foot around in a circle. The bottom hurt, but
not terribly. A cut or at most a good gash. She'd overre-
acted out of surprise, and Caleb—*being Caleb*—jumped
into action more than he needed to.

She started to pull her arm away from around his neck.
"I think I'm fine to walk. The cut doesn't feel deep."

"There was a lot of blood, Paige. I've got you."

Right, and there was also a lot of blood every time she
nicked her ankle shaving, but that didn't require hero in-
tervention. "You don't have to carry me."

"I'm fine. I want to."

"I'm really okay."

"I'd rather be overcautious and keep your foot clean."

A fortress of strength, rock-hard arms bore her weight as he carried her up the sand dune. She was more aware than she wanted to be of his heartbeat against her side.

When he reached where they had been sitting twenty minutes ago, Caleb lowered her so she could scoop up her shoes and socks. In a heartbeat he picked her up again. She used one hand to balance her shoes on her stomach, the other still looped around his neck. The hair on the back of his head brushed against her wrist with each step.

Heartbeat. Hair. Try as she might, Paige could no longer ignore this man.

Sweat coated the back of his neck by the time they reached the top of the dune. He still had to make it through the wooded up-and-down trails before they'd reach the parking lot. She shouldn't let Caleb carry her the whole way. He had to be tired from driving all day, carrying boxes and now from lugging her up the dune.

"If you give me a second to slip my shoes back on, I can hobble for a while." She moved her arm to start to get down. "I'll manage."

"I'm fine." His hold tightened. "I've got you."

Focus on the trees. Focus on the spiderwebs. Focus on anything besides how good his arms felt around her and how he smelled like pine trees and hard work.

Through the canopy, evening sunlight traced warm lines over her face and shoulders. A burning orange flame, the sun began to sink behind them into the lake.

Mostly Caleb kept his eyes on the trail as he stepped over tree roots and navigated a few steady declines, but Paige caught him examining her a few times, his brow low, worried.

Finally he spoke, softly. "I'm sorry about this."

"About what?" Paige turned her head to meet his eyes. Yikes! Too close. Only a few inches away, if she wanted to she could lay her head on his shoulder or rest her forehead against the side of his face. Or kiss his cheek.

Not good.

He glanced at her for the umpteenth time. "I shouldn't have told you to go on the beach without your shoes. If I hadn't—"

Every muscle in her body stiffened. "Excuse me. I must be going crazy, because I thought I just heard you try to take the blame for my foot getting barely hurt."

The side of his jaw popped. "It is—"

"And I know you wouldn't do that because a random accident can't be anyone's fault. Hence the word *accident*." She tapped on his shoulder.

He now focused on the path. "But I told you not to put your shoes on."

"Last time I checked, I'm a grown adult and I make my own choices. You're not allowed to take the blame for this or anything else that ever happens to me. Got it?"

"But—"

"No. End of discussion. I made a choice, and I got hurt. The end." Paige fought the urge to push out of his hold. Piling unneeded guilt onto his own plate over something so silly. The nerve.

Thankfully they'd reached the parking lot or else she would have sprung from his hold and stomped away— bleeding foot notwithstanding.

Caleb must have left his truck unlocked because he opened the passenger door and set her down on the seat without having to pull out his keys.

"One second," he mumbled. He rounded the truck, opened a tub in the back and pulled out a beach towel. "This is clean. Promise." He wrapped it around her injured foot. Hopefully it would stop any more blood.

After starting up the truck and maneuvering out of the

park, Caleb fiddled with the temperature controls. Paige caught him stealing worried glances at her.

At the stoplight, he scrubbed his hand over his face. "I can't help feeling like this shouldn't have happened. We should have gone right back to Maggie's. If I hadn't suggested the dunes then—"

"It's not your fault." Paige let out an exasperated breath. Had it been Bryan with her, he would have blamed her for being careless. Then again, Caleb saying it was his fault proved almost more annoying. "Stop making a big deal about this. If I had been alone right now, I would have put my shoes and socks on and gone home. No big deal."

"I know you said…but I'm replaying it in my mind. You started to put your shoes on and I told you not to. What would it have cost me to wait another minute?"

"Okay. I don't know how everyone around you stands it, but I'm sick of this." She crossed her arms and turned in her seat to face him more. "Let's get one thing straight."

From talking to Maggie and Shelby, and from things Caleb said, he had a bad habit of claiming guilt and piling it up on his shoulders. Only to drag him down unnecessarily. It was ridiculous. The whole town might take it easy on him. They could all keep their secret promise of solidarity in pity. They could all just let Caleb continue on, never growing through their challenges, but Paige wouldn't stand for that.

"Nothing that has or will happen to me is your fault."

"Paige," he groaned.

"Don't talk. I haven't lived here that long, but I've already noticed how much this whole town coddles you." She held up both her hands in the stop gesture when he tried to speak. "Well, I'm not going to let you lay claim to responsibilities that aren't yours just so you can live under your little black rain cloud feeling bad for things that had nothing to do with you."

Caleb stared out the windshield and focused on the road ahead as if he drove through a snowstorm instead of a cloudless, early-fall sunset. Maybe calling him a black rain cloud had gone too far. After all, he usually seemed happy and willing to joke. It wasn't like he walked around town moping. More that everyone treated him like he should. Like he might suddenly break.

Surrounded by potted mums, the sign for Goose Harbor Immediate Care seemed more cheerful than it should.

"Why are we here?" Paige balked.

"Stay in the seat. I don't want you trying to walk on that foot until we have it checked out. Please, humor me on this." Caleb pulled into the nearest open spot, shut his door harder than normal and rounded the truck to get her.

An elderly nurse, capped with a cloudy puff of white hair and a tight smile, showed them to a small exam room. She sported a purple smock covered with giraffes wearing sunglasses. The nurse inspected the cut and muttered under her breath as she wrapped the foot in a loose piece of gauze. She took Paige's vitals before assuring them the doctor would be in soon.

Caleb fiddled with the magazines on a side table in the closet-size room. "There's a Bible here." He offered her the worn book. When she didn't take it right away, he sat back down and leafed through the pages. "It might help take your mind off your foot."

Paige bit her lip. "Honestly? I have the hardest time reading the Bible sometimes. Don't get me wrong, I want to be good at it, but I feel like it's this impossible puzzle that doesn't even make sense."

"It doesn't have to be that way." His fingers moved over the Bible in a light caress. "For a time...I used to hate reading it. Then one day it hit me." He closed the book. "Do you like to get letters in the mail?"

"I've always wanted one—a real one." She shifted on the exam table, making the white cover paper crinkle. "My whole life I've never gotten a letter."

"You're kidding me."

"I got junk mail and bills and everything like that. But a handwritten note addressed to me? Nope."

"Really? Well, I promise I'll send you one someday." He tapped the Bible again, back on track. "If you had gotten one, wouldn't you have treasured it? You wouldn't have gone to your mailbox only to decide not to open it or said 'I'll read that later.' Am I right?"

"Are you kidding me?" She sat up a little straighter. "I would have run with it to my bedroom and ripped the envelope open and savored every word. Back in the day, I would have tacked it to the board above my desk."

He laughed, his eyes lighting up. "Okay, and it probably would have been tenfold that if it was a love letter."

She nodded. Yes, it would have been nice to receive a real love letter. Maybe someday.

"Here's the kicker—this book here, this is a letter that God wrote to you. It's a love letter. I figure each day I choose not to spend time reading what He's written me would be like getting a letter in the mail and deciding not to open it."

"That's a neat way to look at it." Paige reached for the Bible and flipped the pages so it fanned out in her lap. "I like it."

"No charge. That one's free today."

Their gazes met and held.

Wrong move.

She shoved her hands under her thighs to keep them from reaching out for his hand.

Despite the confusion slowly creeping into her heart, she couldn't risk falling for another man again. Even a seemingly nice one whose voice calmed her and who treated her gently was out of the question. Because when push came to shove, even though he was nice about it, Caleb was just one more controlling man. He could say he was keeping her from danger, but overreacting about the cut reminded her of the truth. She wasn't about to chance another man making her feel like Bryan had, which is why she'd constructed such a stronghold over her heart.

So much for impenetrable.

All it had taken was a kind man with warm eyes and a determined will to swoop right on in. She had to protect her heart better. Fairy tales that involve handsome and gallant men like Caleb didn't last long in real life.

She turned her head to shoo away the buzzing thoughts.

A soft knock at the door saved her from any more conversation. An older doctor looked over her foot before starting a slow process of dabbing at the cut to clean it. "You're fortunate—the glass didn't cut you deep at all. In fact, this doesn't need stitches. Looks like I can apply antibacterial cream and a bandage and you'll be right as rain."

Paige shot Caleb a told-you-so look.

The doctor opened a drawer and pulled out a sample tube of cream. He handed it to Paige. "The foot has a lot of capillaries in it so any sort of cut will bleed a lot. Just keep it clean for the next few days. I'd say no socks until Wednesday. Other than that, you can use it as normal."

"So I can go running?" Paige gingerly slipped her tennis shoe onto the injured foot and then stuffed her socks in her pocket.

The doctor nodded. "It's a basic surface cut. Let pain be your guide, but I'd say by Wednesday you'll be fine to jog on it." He touched the screen of a computer tablet he carried and looked over the information. "Looks like you had a tetanus booster not that long ago, so we don't even need to do that. If you don't have any questions you're good to go."

Caleb didn't offer to carry her out to the truck, but he did hold open every door along the way. Without his assistance, Paige climbed into the truck's cab, albeit, quite ungracefully.

With the keys still dangling from his hand, Caleb stared out the window, a glazed-over look in his eyes.

He cleared his throat. "I need to get better at this."

"At what?" Paige buckled her seat belt.

Caleb adjusted to face her. She swallowed hard, biting the edge of her lip, trying to focus on anything but tumbling headfirst into that delicious liquid-chocolate stare.

"You were right—what you said about the people in town. They coddle me. I don't like it. I've noticed that they treat me differently, but I never could pinpoint the right word for it."

"I'm sorry. I shouldn't have—"

"But you're right. They watch me like I'm a dormant volcano that could come to life at any moment." He braced a hand on his head. "I'm not an angry person...I've never been someone like that. So if they're not worried about an eruption, then it's that they're worried I'm going to fall apart, and that's worse. Much worse."

"Hey," Paige whispered, and instinctively rested her hand on his knee. "You've been through a lot. I don't think anyone blames you for acting like that."

His hand dropped so it covered hers. The touch seemed to ground him. With their hands still touching, he leaned his head back on the seat rest. "I need to stop trying to control outcomes for the people I care about."

She straightened up in her seat. It was like he'd been listening in on her thoughts.

"I'm not good at talking about spiritual stuff, but the way I see it is that God cares about those people way more than you do, and they're in His hands. You have to trust them to His care."

"And if they die?" He turned his head her way.

"Then you keep on trusting them to His care."

They drove back to the inn without turning on the radio.

Caleb glanced at her, almost as if he was nervous to talk. "You go on inside and I'll take care of your boxes. I know you and the doctor think I'm overreacting, but I'd feel better if you didn't put extra weight on that foot tonight."

"Actually, I'm tired, so I'm going to take you up on that offer."

He put the car in Park and relaxed his hold on the wheel as she opened the passenger-side door. "I just wanted to say that even though we haven't known each other long, I'm thankful to have you in my life."

Paige nodded and took a step back into the shadows to mask the grateful tears that threatened to fall. "I'm thankful for you, too."

And she was.

Chapter Eleven

Caleb watched the steam rise from his coffee mug and caught Maggie staring at him from the other side of the booth. After running into her at church, they'd decided to stop by Cherry Top for lunch together.

"I know that expression, Mags." He gripped the coffee mug. Too hot. "What are you cooking up in that mind of yours?"

She dabbed her mouth with one of the thin napkins from the small box on the table. "I'm thinking I know you too well."

He blew on his coffee before taking a sip. "And what's that supposed to mean?"

Maggie leaned forward. "It means I know you like Paige, so don't you go trying to deny it."

Like Paige? He hadn't considered feelings until now.

Okay, that wasn't true. He'd known yesterday when he held her in his arms outside her childhood home that he was already in deep. Feelings had grown before he'd known they were there. Hearing about her past hurts when they were at the beach had only served to further strengthen the bond he felt with her.

With her clean girl-next-door looks and bright blue eyes,

it would have been difficult not to like Paige. His mind leafed through files of images in his head—the first day he met her, tearstained and helpless, to her refusing to back down to him about Sarah's Home. The picture shouldn't fit, but maybe that's why she appealed to him. There was more to her than a need for a man. Paige had an independence that allowed Caleb to let down his guard around her. Besides yesterday with her ex-fiancé, he didn't *have* to protect her or do anything for her. She didn't need him, but somehow that made him like her more.

Caleb glanced at the ceiling. The spackle looked like white measles. Then he met Maggie's eyes and let out a long, deep breath. "Sure I like her. What's not to like?"

"Do you really mean that?" Maggie wore a goofy grin and bounced in her seat.

Caleb rested his hand on the back of the booth cushion. "She's great with the students, and even though I don't want her coming to Sarah's Home, when she's there and at the high school, she's always willing to pitch in with any type of work. She's thoughtful and doesn't just talk for the sake of talking." He paused.

"Like how I do all the time?" Maggie laughed.

Maggie and Shelby both talked a mile a minute and often for no other benefit than to fill the airspace and avoid silence. As much as he loved them both, the constant chatter sometimes wore on him. However, Paige seemed comfortable with silence. Which was refreshing.

He ignored Maggie. "Know what else I appreciate about Paige? When she talks to me she's not worried about hurting my feelings and there's no pity in her actions."

Maggie's smile fell. "I don't—"

"You do."

Maggie snaked a hand toward his and covered it for a moment on the table. "I'm sorry. Truly. It's just…when it first happened, I didn't know what to say, and it kept being like that."

"I know you don't do it on purpose." Caleb slipped his hand away and leaned back against the booth. "Everyone in town does it. To them, I'm defined by what happened on one day of my life. There is nothing else they think when they look at me."

"I don't know if that's true." Even as she spoke, Maggie gave him the look a person gives an old dog with an under bite who's just been surrendered to an animal shelter.

He looked out the window at the ship masts bobbing in the marina. "It feels true. But Paige doesn't look at me that way. In fact, I think she's the only one with the gumption to go toe-to-toe with me. It's refreshing."

"Are you going to ask her out?"

"No. I couldn't." He straightened and looked back at Maggie. "It's not like that."

"Why not?"

"Paige deserves better, and besides, I don't have the available time to give to a relationship or a woman in order to make her a priority. A woman like Paige should have that. Between my time at school and church and Sarah's Home—I can't give her a relationship in the way she deserves." Caleb shifted in his seat. He had said too much already.

Shelby always told him that a person makes time for what they value. And she was right. If Caleb looked honestly at his time, he'd already started placing value on the moments spent with Paige. Between finding reasons to stop by her classroom, swinging by Maggie's on a daily basis and seeking her out at Sarah's Home, Paige was already a priority in his life.

Caleb had to face the facts—he *was* considering starting a new relationship. A month ago he would have said that would never happen. How had Paige worked her way into his mind and heart in the past few weeks without his permission?

"Listen." He tossed a few bills on the table and scooted out of the booth. "Don't talk about this to anyone. Especially not to Paige. Okay, Mags…I know how you are. I probably shouldn't have said anything."

Maggie walked out the front door with him and grabbed his elbow before they parted ways for the day. "Paige has been through a lot, too. She's broken like you are, but I really believe you two would fit well together. Just be patient with her, okay? She's going to be really slow to trust a man and she needs time."

He yanked the baseball hat out of his back pocket and put it on. "Like I said, I'm not going to act on anything I just told you."

"Trust me." Maggie winked at him. "You will."

Caleb jammed his hands into his pockets and took the long route home. Perhaps it was time to date again. He'd made peace with Sarah's memory a long time ago. He didn't believe dating meant he was betraying her memory—that was never how Sarah had been. She would have encouraged him to find love and a family more than a year ago.

Okay. What if he let himself care about Paige? And what if something terrible happened? It was safer—better—to stay in his house with Shelby and occasionally check on Maggie and add no one else to his list of responsibilities. Although, love wasn't a responsibility—it was a gift. No one hems and haws over being given a gift.

He stopped in his tracks. Love? He didn't love Paige—didn't know her well enough for a claim like that. It had taken him more than ten years of friendship with Sarah to admit to loving her. Love happened slowly. But he couldn't deny the pull he felt toward Paige.

He needed to get home, change and go for a jog. That was the only possible way to calm his thoughts and refocus on the normal rhythm of his life. He picked up his pace to get home quicker.

Maggie had pressed his buttons, and he needed a reminder that he was better off alone.

Caleb worked the pen around and around between his fingers.

She showed up at Sarah's Home, even after he told her she might not want to come with a hurt foot. Paige told him earlier she'd been running on it and everything was healing, but it didn't stem his worry. The quarters were tight here and she might get stepped on or jostled. What if the cut on her foot started bleeding again or became infected?

Stop controlling other people's outcomes.

Setting down the pen, he willed his shoulders to relax by rolling them a couple of times. He watched Paige perform a secret handshake with one of the students and high-five the next three in the homework room. She walked without a limp.

Stop worrying. She's fine. Knowing Paige, she could dance on that foot.

Principal Timmons handed Caleb a stack of note cards. "She's not half-bad at this, is she?"

"As much as you know I don't want to, I'm going to have to concede that you were right about her. Paige has a way with these students." Caleb shuffled through the note cards. "Did you know she's convinced four of them to apply for college and has helped two of them fill out scholarship paperwork?"

What an amazing woman.

Timmons called for the close of the evening just as Caleb inched closer to where Paige worked at a large table with three of the older teens. She didn't rush the students out. Instead she finished answering their questions, hugged each one goodbye and stayed to clean up.

Noticing the computers on the edge of the room still glowed, Caleb used turning them off as an excuse to stay in the room with her. For some reason lately, he found himself gravitating to wherever she was. Whether at school functions, around town or at Sarah's Home—he just ended up in the same room with her.

Man, he was acting like a fifteen-year-old with a crush on the cute new transfer student.

His hand stilled over the computer mouse.

"Do you know his name is Albert?" Paige's voice was a welcome interruption to his thoughts.

"Who?" Caleb clicked the shutdown button on the last computer before joining her at the table.

"Smalls." She grinned.

Caleb dropped into a chair. "I've known him for four years and he wouldn't tell me or anyone his name. How'd you get him to do that?"

Paige shrugged. "I went to one of his slam-poetry sessions on Sunday."

"Alone?" The word sprang out of his mouth before he could stop it.

She narrowed her eyes. "We talked about this, buster. You were going to cut the superman-slash-nosy-old-man business. Remember, it's God's job to take care of people."

He raised his hands in surrender. "Old habit. But do me a favor and tell me if you go again—not for why you're thinking. I'd actually really like to see Smalls in action." He gave her a smile he hoped exuded sincerity.

Paige beamed at him, causing his heart to pound against his rib cage like a hyper dog stuck behind a fence.

Okay, he liked Paige. A lot. Suddenly, Principal Timmons's order to chaperone the Barn Dance didn't sound all that bad. Not if he could convince Paige to attend with him. Although, he didn't know her well enough yet to know if she'd like something like that.

Timmons popped his head in the room. "The front door is locked and I'm heading out for the evening."

They both waved goodbye. Paige started to gather her belongings, piling books and notepads into a canvas bag. Next, she scooped up a couple of jump drives that held a few of the students' essays for their college applications. She'd offered to take them home to read and edit their work.

Caleb held out his hand to carry her bag. "You're great with these students."

Paige slipped on her zip-up hooded sweatshirt and grabbed her car keys. "They're fun to work with."

"They can be. Some of our old volunteers left because they said the students were draining or unreachable. But for you it's second nature. A lot of people who have served here are doing it because they feel like they should, but you were born to do this sort of thing. There's a difference."

"How about you, Caleb? Were you born to do this?"

As if his tongue had been coated in peanut butter, it stuck in his mouth.

Did he really care about these students in the same way Paige did?

Sarah had. They'd started Sarah's Home because she'd wanted it—this had been her passion. Not his. He'd loved seeing his wife excited, but without her, he would have never ended up serving in the capacity he did now.

He enjoyed his students in Goose Harbor and seemed to have a much bigger impact with them than those that filtered in and out of Sarah's Home. Sure, he mentored students at the nonprofit every year, but when he left Brookside all thoughts of the students here left his mind, as well.

He'd stayed after Sarah's death to honor her. She would have wanted to see the place continue to flourish. When the mayor threatened to shut Sarah's Home down, Caleb made it his mission to convince city council otherwise. For Sarah. After he won, he had to stay. How would it have looked if he walked away after that? Staying had been the expected thing, and if there was one thing Caleb could be counted on for, it was to do the expected.

Pursing her lips, Paige studied him. "That wasn't supposed to be a trick question."

"I know." He locked the back door after they walked out. "But I can't answer it in a way that I'm comfortable with."

She nodded. "It's okay not to have all the answers." Paige eased the bag off his shoulder—her touch like sparklers all over his skin. "Sometimes it's better that way."

"Maybe." He glanced back at the dark building.

Her Mazda chirped, letting him know she was about to leave, but then he felt her hand on his wrist. He looked at her.

Paige's smile was soft. "What you do here—it's a good thing, Caleb. Don't diminish the impact you have—no matter what the reason." She squeezed his arm before letting go.

He swallowed hard, working up courage. "Do you want to go somewhere together? We could grab some coffee and talk."

"Not tonight." She fought back a yawn. "I'm supposed to make a ton of scones for Maggie's inn. I should have done them early. I'm going to be up so late."

Long after she left, he stayed, his arms crossed as he

leaned against his truck. Should he continue spending his time here? He'd never considered leaving before.

Maybe Sarah's Home didn't need him anymore.

Paige flipped the lights on in Maggie's kitchen and pulled an apron over her head. She went through the ritual of pulling out flour, eggs, butter. Good for Maggie, taking the night off. If anyone deserved time off, it was her.

Tomorrow at school Paige would kick herself for being up this late, but she'd solve that with copious amounts of coffee.

She began measuring out ingredients.

Ever since Paige had made a batch of her cranberry white chocolate scones her first week in town for Maggie to serve to tourists staying at her inn, they had become one of the most requested menu items. They were a lot of work to make, but Paige was happy to be able to give back to Maggie in this small way. Hadn't she opened up her home and her heart to Paige? Maggie offered the branch of friendship when Paige had most needed it. The least Paige could do was bake some of her secret-recipe scones.

"Can I help?" A deep voice only a few feet behind her made her jump.

Paige yelped, twisting around, and collided with Caleb's rock-hard chest. She really needed to start locking Maggie's back door. Although, knowing Caleb, he probably had a key to the inn.

"Whoa, careful there." He wrapped his arms around her so she wouldn't fall.

Paige's lungs couldn't take in enough air as her heart hammered in her ears. It shouldn't feel so right to be in this man's arms—but it did. Moving out of his grasp, she silently ordered the butterflies in her stomach to curl up and die.

"Were you looking for Maggie?" Paige edged farther away from him and started chopping frozen butter into her mix. She chanced a glance back at him, which of course was a big mistake.

Stop, Paige! The feeling had to go away. She didn't want a man in her life. Especially this one—this one that made her believe in a different possibility for the future than the one she had recently imagined. He had no right to smile at her like he was right now. All calm and assuring. It was singularly disarming.

Caleb ran his hand under his collar, working out knots in his neck. "No. I didn't come for her. I came for you."

"If you came to distract me, I'm not going to allow it. You hear?" Paige jutted the goopy spoon toward him while she laughed.

"Easy there, Trigger." He put his hands up in mock surrender. "After you told me about the scones at Sarah's Home, I figured I'd come by and help. Maybe we can get them done faster if we're both working. Where does Maggie keep the aprons?"

Paige bit her lip and squinted one eye, assessing him. "Deal. But only if I get to pick out which apron."

Without waiting for consent, she fished the pink tulip apron out of the drawer and looped it over Caleb's head. He broke into his brilliant smile.

Where had *this* Caleb emerged from? The Caleb she'd met a few weeks ago always had a worried brow, not a ready laugh. This joking side of Caleb was a welcome change. Why didn't he act like this more often?

"Wow. This is quite the apron. Tie it for me?" He turned around for her, and she put a hand on his back. She shouldn't have been surprised by how firm his muscles were, but she was.

He turned back around, reached behind her, his arm grazing her side, and pulled the bowl closer to stir.

"You're going to have to do that with your hands soon. It gets a little flaky. Here. Just dump it onto the counter and knead in the chips and cranberries." Paige demonstrated.

He bumped her out of the way with his hip and took over. "I know a little about working in the kitchen. My mom used to draft me for help all the time when Shelby and I were kids."

She started another bowl going and adjusted the oven to the right temperature. Turning her own mixture out she began kneading, and then puffed at her hair which slipped into her vision. She chided herself for forgetting to pull it up. Suddenly, Caleb's fingers, featherlight, were on her face—brushing the hair behind her ears before she could process what was happening.

"Whoops. I promise I was trying to be nice." The corner of his mouth tipped up. He showed her his doughy hands that must have left a trail of flour all over her face. She grabbed a handful of flour and tossed it at him, but he lunged out of the way, rounding the sink then spinning around—spray faucet in hand to face his opponent.

"Go ahead and try me," he challenged. "You can't get out of here without walking past me, and you take one step forward and you'll get it."

"Weren't you supposed to be helping me?"

He raised an eyebrow.

"You wouldn't spray that in Maggie's kitchen."

"Try me." He grinned.

"Okay, okay. I surrender." Paige dropped the flour. She managed a defeated smile and went back to kneading.

"Not so quick. While I have you cornered, say you'll go

with me to the Barn Dance tomorrow. And just a hint—" he twirled the spray faucet in his hand "—I'm not taking no for an answer."

"I don't know how to square-dance. Aren't the chaperones supposed to be instructors?" Paige pushed her hair out of her eyes with the back of her hand.

"I'll teach you. Tomorrow evening. It'll be fun."

"I don't know." Trying to hide the warmth spreading over her cheeks, she turned away. The chance to spend more time with Caleb—this joking, smiling version of Caleb—made her want to say yes, but she couldn't dance. A rabid squirrel would have been a better dance partner than her.

He still had the spray faucet in his hand, but his smile dimmed. "You're cleared by your doctor for your foot, right?"

She nodded. "I've already been running on it just fine."

"Oh. Um." He hooked the nozzle back on the sink and kept his back to her. "That's fine if you don't want to go with me. I just thought…"

Maggie told her he hadn't asked anyone out on a date since Sarah. Not that being a cochaperone to the Barn Dance counted as a date. But still, if she turned him down for this it could set him back if he did want to start dating women again. An image of Amy rose in her head, and her stomach twisted at the thought of him asking her instead.

Okay, if she was being honest, she wanted to go with Caleb. Very much. If only saying yes didn't require dancing.

But better to make a fool of herself with him than sit at home wondering all night who he was dancing with besides her. Anyway, Tammie, one of her students, had been bugging her to attend since the volleyball tryouts.

Paige pegged him in the shoulder with a small ball of dough. "Get over here and help me. Looks like I need to wake up early tomorrow and learn some square-dance steps."

Chapter Twelve

For the sixth time during practice Paige stumbled. Caleb gave a good-natured smile and offered his hand again. Taking it, Paige tried to remember the steps. If only she could will her feet to move correctly.

The song skipped on the old record player Lenny the Leech had set up on a wobbly table in the gym for them. Blue padded mats lined the walls and the smell of old sweat hung in the air. Good thing the Barn Dance wouldn't be held here tonight.

Every other pair had their dance down pat; only Paige and Caleb still fumbled. And it had nothing to do with Caleb.

Caleb could have expertly taught each step at the Barn Dance.

With a weak smile, Paige looked down and tried to move her feet at the right time, but that only lasted a half a second before treading right on his foot.

"Ouch!" He stopped moving. "Now you might want to try aiming for the left foot next time. That right one's taken a beating from you already today," he joked.

Biting her quivering lip, Paige tried to meet his eyes, but she couldn't fake a smile. This was nothing short of humiliating, and on top of that, she was supposed to teach high-school students these steps tonight.

She shouldn't have said yes. Caleb should be with someone who matched him better. Hadn't Principal Timmons called Sarah an irreplaceable woman? Paige had no right entertaining the feelings for him that swirled in her heart. But Caleb's smile today was infectious, and the way he patiently praised her efforts had made a seed of hope take root in her heart. The way he watched out for her was so different from the men in her past. As she looked back on the past month, even when he tried to overprotect, he did it in a way that made her feel cherished. Caleb encouraged the best in her.

Yet here she was, probably disappointing him. He'd wanted one evening to have fun at the dance, and she couldn't even remember the steps.

Caleb reached for her hand, but Paige held up hers to stop him. Pinching the bridge of her nose to stop the rush of tears, she chided herself.

Why was she making such a big deal of this? Yes, she felt foolish because she couldn't master something so simple. That was partly the reason, but another big part of it was Caleb. In prayer, she'd told God she didn't want a man in her life right now. Then all of a sudden the right one stood in front of her, reaching out his hand with a slight smile spreading across his face.

"What are you thinking right now? That furled brow doesn't bode well for us." Caleb reached over and squeezed her shoulder.

"I…I can't do this." Paige hung her head and continued, "I'm not going to get the moves down by tonight. Does Maggie know it already? Wouldn't you rather dance with her? Everyone knows her, and it won't be weird that she's at a school thing. I'll still come as a chaperone if that's the issue."

He didn't answer right away. Taking his hand from her shoulder he moved it to cup her chin and drew her face up so their eyes locked. He looked intensely at her for a moment. "But I want to dance with you."

She swallowed hard. "Maybe you should dance with Amy." Saying the words hurt, but knowing Amy, she could probably do the dances in her sleep.

Caleb's lips twitched. "Maybe not."

Paige pulled out of his hold. "You know, it would probably be a good thing for her. She could use a boost. Some of the teens were saying downright mean things about her the other week. So many of the students respect you—if you showed up with her maybe it would make them be kinder to her." What was wrong with her? Who shoves a good man into the arms of another woman? Evidently Paige Windom.

"Maybe I would, if I was wired another way." He drew in a long breath. "I have nothing against Amy. She's a nice woman, but I can't dance with someone unless I feel something for them. Call me old-fashioned, but even holding hands—that means too much to me to do casually." He offered the hand that a second ago had cradled her chin.

Paige slipped her hand into his. Did her action mean as much to him as it did to her? "But we'd be dancing, so what's the difference?"

He just raised his eyebrows and spun her in a circle. Did that mean…?

The song changed and another one of the science teachers called out for a promenade.

Caleb gave her hand a light tug, letting her know to step out for the group of couples they practiced with. He led her to the edge of the gym.

"Do you know what the issue is, Paige?"

She shrugged.

"It's not that you can't do this. It's that you're looking at the situation all wrong."

"I am?"

"You keep watching the other people around you. You watch your own feet. Comparing yourself to others and focusing on yourself—those things will only ever lead to stumbling. Sure, you can fake that you know what you're doing for a little while, but when others are looking to you for help…they'll catch on eventually."

"Then what am I supposed to do? I don't want to make a fool of myself tonight."

He offered her both his hands, palms up. "I know the dance. Trust that I can lead you. Can you do that?"

"But how?" she whispered.

"Do you trust me?"

She bit her lip. Did he know what he was asking—how difficult that was for her?

But a thought rushed through her. She could trust Caleb. Really.

She nodded.

"Then look right at my face the whole time, and I promise, everything else will follow."

"Wake up, you big lug."

Caleb woke up to Maggie poking him in the arm. Lifting his head, he looked around in a startled, groggy haze. Between practice for the Barn Dance that morning and then cleaning the gutters at Maggie's inn afterward, he'd been beat. He'd thought to rest on the living-room couch a few minutes before going home.

He blinked a couple of times. Must have fallen asleep.

"Earth to Caleb." Maggie waved her hands in front of

his face. "You have a barn dance to get ready for. I'm kicking you out."

"I just need to change." He yawned. "It won't take me that long."

Maggie pulled a face that bunched up her nose. "As your friend, I'm going to say that you don't smell the best right now so you best head home and shower."

Sitting up, he good-naturedly rolled his eyes.

Maggie popped her hands onto her hips. "I need you out anyway so I can get Cinderella ready."

"Where's Paige?" He stretched his hands above his head and tried to shake the soreness out of his arms and back. He'd hurt tonight after working on the gutters.

"I made her go start getting ready. You do realize you're going to have to fight the other single guys off tonight after I'm done with her."

He scrubbed his hand down his face. "Just where did you two disappear to after practice this morning anyway?"

"I took her shopping. We went clear out to the mall in Shadowbend, and then we got caught up talking. Girl stuff." She winked. "I shouldn't tell you, but you did come up in conversation. And for the record—Paige spent a good five minutes in here watching you sleep until I forced her to go take a shower."

"Really?" Caleb lifted an eyebrow, unsure if Maggie was teasing him or trying to slyly relay vital information.

"Uh-huh. She kept saying—" at this, Maggie raised her voice to imitate Paige "—'How is it that guys look so cute when they're sleeping?'"

He stood up, grabbed his wallet off the coffee table and tucked it into his back pocket. "Well, that's one way to ruin a guy's day. Call him cute."

"*Cute* is good!"

"*Cute* is a word used for puppy dogs and little kids."

"You're impossible. Get out of here, buddy. I expect you back in an hour looking every bit a gentleman."

"Aye, aye, Captain." Caleb saluted her and took the hint.

Sitting out in his truck before turning it on, he wondered what the night could possibly hold.

For the first time in two years he was actually looking forward to the Barn Dance.

He should have brought flowers. That was the customary practice for something like this. A man brings his date flowers on an occasion that calls for someone needing an hour to get ready.

But this wasn't a date.

She'd hesitated so long before saying yes, and even then it was because she was under threat of getting sprayed with water. He shook his head. What had gotten in to him? He was acting like a flirtatious teenager.

For tonight, whatever the reason for Paige Windom saying yes, Caleb was thankful.

It's not a date. He kept repeating the words to himself on the way over to the West Oaks Inn.

Hopefully Maggie wouldn't make a big deal over it— yanking out the camera and making them stand awkwardly together taking mock prom pictures. She'd done that so many times when he'd showed up for Sarah over the years.

As his truck bumped up the gravel driveway, his greatest fears were confirmed. Maggie and Shelby—*why was she there?*—waited for him. His stomach dropped. What if the attention scared Paige? He'd have to put a stop to it. Walk in and whisk Paige out as quickly as possible.

"Ooh, is that a new top?" Shelby fussed as he crossed the lawn. "I love you in that straw cowboy hat. The students will be putting your handsome mug all over Instagram."

Whatever Shelby's reason for showing up and meddling, he'd talk to her tonight. No reason getting into a discussion here with the possibility of Paige overhearing.

He sidestepped his sister. "Where's Paige? We need to head out."

At that exact moment she walked out the front door and the sight of her made his heart take off like a fugitive in a high-speed car chase. For all Caleb knew, someone had sucker punched him in the gut. His lungs couldn't take in enough air.

Most of the students and faculty dressed for the Barn Dance in jeans and flannel shirts. Paige wore a long skirt that flowed when she walked, shiny new boots and a shirt that cinched at her small waist.

Beautiful didn't describe her. It couldn't. It didn't mean enough. She was stunning—smiling, the deep blue pools of her eyes luminous, her hair spilling down her back in large, loose, golden curls—and walking straight toward him.

Caleb tried to swallow the lump in his throat. She was his date. This gorgeous woman who enchanted him, teased him and challenged him on a daily basis. This beauty that, unbeknownst to her, was making him a better man—making him face things he'd locked away two years ago—was his.

At least for tonight.

"You look great." Caleb managed.

Giving him a lazy smile she shrugged. "I feel weird. I think Maggie has it out for me." Pulling her gauzy skirt up a couple of inches, she showed off her shoes. "Look at how high the heels are on these boots. I'm not used to walking in these babies yet, and now I'm supposed to dance in them."

"Just hang on to me tonight." Caleb offered his hand and gestured toward his truck.

"You two are so cute." Shelby busted in between them, looping an arm through each of theirs. Dropping her voice she said, "You owe me for doing damage control—I made Maggie promise not to embarrass you guys with pictures. She fought me hard on it, though. And, bro, take care of Paige, I'm afraid all the guys will be after her tonight."

Paige fixed her hair in the visor's mirror and stared at her reflection. There was nothing significant about her. No reason for Caleb to want to be with her.

He had seen her crying, been on the receiving end of her anger, listened to her deepest wounds, stayed with her when she was bleeding and hadn't laughed at her when she voiced doubts about God and the Bible. All that, and he kept choosing to spend time with her.

His cowboy-themed button-down shirt molded across his athletic shoulders as fading sunlight poured through the window, giving his brown hair a shimmery aspect. Clean shaven, he glanced at her shyly out of the corner of his eye.

In a small town, it didn't take long to reach a destination. He pulled into the parking lot of the country club and then rounded the truck to help her down.

She braced her hand on the side of his truck. "These shoes really were a terrible idea."

"You can take them off when we get inside. Most everyone ends up dancing barefoot anyway."

"Okay, before we go in there can you answer one question for me?"

"Shoot."

"This is not a barn."

"Please form that into a question and I'll answer you." He smiled.

"Why is this thing held in a country club if it's called a Barn Dance?"

"Easy. It got too big to hold in the barn owned by the forest preserve and none of the people with barns on their private property want the whole student body trampling around on their yard."

Caleb offered her his arm as they walked into the Barn Dance.

Her student Tammie ran up to them and snapped a picture without warning. "I didn't know you guys were dating! Sorry, Mr. Beck, but my friend is going to be devastated when I show her this picture. She's had a crush on you since last year."

Paige bit her lip. She should probably correct Tammie before she spread that she and Caleb were a couple all over the school.

Tammie squealed. "But you two are so cute together. Nice work snagging him, Miss W." She glanced at the digital image on the back of her camera. "This is so making it into the yearbook." She rushed off.

Heat raced to Paige's cheeks. "The students can be so… energetic."

Caleb chuckled. "Especially the girls."

The room was cavernous with high ceilings lined with exposed mahogany beams. The wood floor gleamed, and the back wall boasted floor-to-ceiling glass with an overview of the rolling, well-manicured golf course. In clear contrast with the building, bales of hay and scarecrows lined the edge of the room. A giant table in the middle overflowed with a gurgling chocolate fountain, and a live band played old folk songs on the stage.

"You look great." Bree waved at her. She looked cute in a loud print standing beside the lanky IT guy who worked in the school district's administration building.

"You, too," Paige mouthed as she and Caleb moved across the room.

After the next song concluded, Principal Timmons took the stage and announced the start of square dancing. "The chaperones will run through the first two songs and then everyone else can form squares and join."

"Ready?" Caleb pumped her hand.

"I guess I have to be." Paige grinned at him.

They launched into the first song, and Paige did what Caleb had asked her—she trusted he could lead her. She looked right at his face the whole time. There were a few missed steps, but they laughed it off, and judging by the applause at the end of the second demonstration, no one in the crowd minded.

Caleb led her off the floor.

Bree flashed a toothy grin. "You did good, kid."

"I missed a couple steps."

"Eh. We all do. I always think dancing is like life in a way, and I like to picture God as my dance partner leading me in all sorts of new and fun steps. Sometimes I mess it up, but He's right there to catch me in the midst of those stumbles." Bree waved. "I have to go.... Don't want any girls flirting with my cute IT guy."

After a few songs the square dancing morphed into normal teenage dancing, which consisted of students standing in circles, shuffling their feet and raising their hands in the air every once in a while. Paige and Caleb made the rounds for their official chaperone duties and checked the hallways for mischief. Students kept asking to take pictures with them.

Caleb squeezed Paige's hand. "I have to go make the announcement for Barn Dance king and queen."

"I think I'll grab some fresh air while you do that." Paige stepped outside and breathed in the crisp evening air.

I know the dance. Trust that I can lead you. Can you do that?

Caleb spoke the words earlier today, but she knew now that they applied to her relationship with God. For too long she'd pictured God above the world, too worried about everything else to consider her life, but it changed everything to imagine Him this way—reaching out His hand, asking her to trust Him.

"You care about me, don't You?" she whispered to the night sky.

Hadn't Caleb told her that God gave her worth the moment He created her?

"I trust You." A rush of calm seeped into her heart, untying binds she hadn't even realized were there.

Timmons cornered Caleb before he could make it back to Paige.

"I have a small favor to ask of you." The principal wore a rather large Stetson hat and a huge belt buckle.

"Wasn't me chaperoning this dance a small favor?" He scanned the dance room. Where was Paige, anyway?

Timmons winked at him. "Admit it. You're having a good time."

"Okay." Caleb crossed his arms and shook his head good-naturedly. "What's this favor?"

"I don't know if you heard, but Coach Quinn was rushed to the hospital this afternoon."

"The basketball coach? Is he all right?"

"He'll have to have his gallbladder removed and won't be able to perform his coaching duties for the next few weeks. I asked Lenny, but he can't do it because coaching would interfere with that indoor soccer club he plays in. You're the only one I know on staff who plays besides him, and the boys have an important game this Thursday. League rules are that they must be accompanied by a coach or they have to forfeit. I'd hate to have all the students' hard work go to waste."

Thursday. He'd have to make sure Paige didn't go to Sarah's Home that night. "Sure, I can fill in for him."

"I knew I could count on you." The principal slapped his back.

Caleb turned back to face the main part of the room and spotted Paige right away. She was surrounded by some of the other single male teachers. They were fluttering around her like mosquitos to a bug zapper. If only they would fry when they touched her, it would serve them right. He saw one offer his hand...probably asking her to dance.

Caleb quickened his pace.

If he felt that strongly about seeing her talking to other guys, then it was time to tell her.

Paige excused herself from her present conversation with two other staff members as Caleb started to cross the room.

He glanced at the people she'd been talking with. "Everything okay?"

"Everything's great."

"Were they trying to get you to dance?" He scrubbed his hand over his chin.

She pursed her lips. "Caleb Beck, if I didn't know better I'd say you were jealous."

"Maybe I am." He took a step closer.

"We were brainstorming ideas for the spring musical." She jutted her thumb back toward two of the men—one was the choir director and the other taught journalism. "That's all." She fought a yawn.

"Are you ready to head home? Timmons said he was fine to close the dance without me. It's only got another fifteen minutes until they start clearing out anyway."

"Sure. I'm tired."

He offered his arm and she took it. Her feet were sore from wearing brand-new boots.

They shuffled out to the truck and climbed inside. Caleb laid his arm across the back of the bench, the warmth of his fingers only an inch from touching her neck the whole ride home. Why didn't he just make a move already?

He put his hand back on the wheel to help him steer as the truck bumped its way up Maggie's driveway.

Instead of just dropping her off, he put the truck in Park. "The sky's so clear now. Look at all the stars. Care to watch them with me for a couple minutes?"

"I'd love to." Paige smiled at him through the dim light. He motioned for her to meet him at the back of the truck where he pulled down the tailgate.

He slipped out of his coat and helped her into it. "It's a little colder than I thought."

"Thanks." She cuddled into the warmth of his jacket.

"Let me help you up." Caleb put his hands on her waist and then didn't move.

Not knowing what to say, Paige smoothed her hand down his chest.

He responded by touching his forehead to hers. "There are a million things going through my mind right now, and I can't find the words. I'm so worried something will happen, and this will all disappear. Nothing bad can happen to you," he whispered.

The old Paige would have considered his words bordering on controlling, but she knew Caleb better now. This fear came from the core of his soul and it meant he cared, really cared about her to voice that. It had taken her a lot of mistakes and years to learn that not only men slay dragons, but women were capable of waging battles against other people's greatest fears, as well.

She licked her lips. "But Caleb…if something ever does happen to me—" she gulped "—it's not your fault."

He pulled back and studied her face. "Don't you know by now, I'm crazy about you?"

Paige released an uncharacteristic giggle. "I'm pretty crazy about you, too."

After a deep breath, Caleb squared her face in his hands. He looked her in the eye as he started to lean closer. She swallowed hard, biting the edge of her lip to keep from tumbling headfirst into that delicious, liquid-chocolate stare.

Automatically, she tipped her lips to meet his. She drank him in, lingering in his kiss and savoring the feel of his hands in her hair. It was like nothing she could have imagined. Caleb's kiss was a blessing—a gift that made her feel secure and cherished instead of like something had just been stolen from her.

No more fighting her feelings with this man. It was time to see what an honest relationship looked like.

Chapter Thirteen

She still had a couple of minutes before Caleb would be there to pick her up for a date. Immediately after their kiss last night he'd asked her to go to lunch with him, and of course she said yes.

Paige trailed her fingers over the Bible passage she read in a loving caress. At the church held inside a movie theater that she'd attended with Maggie, the pastor talked about a book of the Bible called the Psalms. When she got home she found a cozy chair on the porch and went back over what she'd learned during the sermon.

Fall slowly crept into Goose Harbor leaving the afternoon cooler than it had been the past couple of weeks. Darker clouds started to roll in over Lake Michigan and a bit of a breeze whistled through the spindly porch rails. The air smelled like rain. Paige tucked the afghan she'd carried outside with her a little tighter around her shoulders and took a sip of the warm mint tea from the mug she balanced on the edge of the handrail.

She really liked this David guy who'd written a large chunk of the Psalms. He wasn't like some of the churchy people she'd come across in life—the ones who told her she had to act perfect all the time. Not at all. David argued with God. David ranted. David cried out and wept. He celebrated with singing and dancing. This man was completely flesh and blood who made a lot of terrible mistakes like anyone else. The only thing that separated him from others was that he loved God. That's it.

But that made all the difference.

He came to God with every aspect of his emotions— ones Paige had always felt like she shouldn't bother God with—yet God called David a man after His own heart.

She reread the words David scrawled so many years ago and let them take root in her mind.

When I am afraid, I will trust in You. In God, whose word I praise, in God I trust.

The porch creaked as Maggie stepped outside with a dish towel over her shoulder. "It's a nice day to read the Bible out of doors, although it looks like we might get some rain tonight." She nodded to indicate the worn book in Paige's lap.

Caleb's truck bumped up the driveway.

Paige pushed out from under her afghan. "I'm going to be honest with you. I've been away from this book for a long time. Actually, I don't know if I ever really read it before."

"Well, that's the best thing about God. Each day is a new chance to start over. You've come to Goose Harbor for a fresh start, and now you can be anyone you want. There's a verse that says just that—God is making everything new and that we can trust what He says. You should look it up." Maggie bowed her head and went back inside the inn.

"Thanks. I will."

Making all things new. Paige liked that. She made a small note on her pad of paper to find that verse later.

"Hey, beautiful." Caleb took the front steps two at a time and grinned at her. "Ready to head out?"

"Let me just put this stuff inside." She started to rise.

He eased the Bible and blanket from her hand. "I'll do it. I want to say hey to Mags."

The moment he walked inside, another vehicle turned into Maggie's driveway. A red BMW spun into the parking lot heaving a spray of gravel and a dust cloud in its wake.

Paige froze.

She knew that car well. Bryan and she had shared their first kiss in that car—a clumsy kiss quickly taken from her after an action movie on their third date.

Still having a hard time believing her ex-fiancé would have any reason to be in Goose Harbor, Paige gripped the railing as she climbed down the porch steps.

Bryan slammed his door and then rounded the car, planting himself in her path.

She didn't want to deal with him again. Never again. Why was he here? "How did you know where to find me?"

"Your mother called. She says you aren't being faithful, Paige. Out with some man last weekend—how would that look for me if the papers got wind of something like that? You could ruin next year's election."

"Well, sorry you wasted the trip, but I have nothing to say to you."

"I'm taking you home." He reached for her.

But she moved away so his hand caught only air.

She prayed for words and courage.

You had worth beyond measure from the moment God created you, and no one can take that away. Not that man. And not your feelings.

Caleb's words rushed back into her mind.

Paige straightened out her spine. "I'm not going anywhere with you."

Bryan's ears turned red and she noticed his right hand shaking.

In the years she'd known Bryan, he had won every fight, every debate. She never had a quick enough answer for him. Days later she would think through conversations and realize what she could have said to change the way the talk had gone, but it had always been too late.

His glare could burn. "You're done playing. You're done making me look like a fool to our friends back home. Got it? You are getting in this car and coming with me. Now." Bryan moved forward and seized her wrist as he spoke.

"Let go. This is where I live." She pawed at his hand but it didn't budge.

Secretly, for that first month after the breakup and when their wedding day came and went, Paige had wished that he would come, just like he was now, and demand to be back with her—to tell her he was sorry and say he wanted to be with her.

But Bryan never said he was sorry—ever—in all the years she had known him.

She had loved his confidence, loved that he always had the answers, but suddenly she couldn't quite see what she had found so attractive about him. Why had she been so stuck on this man? He was certainly good-looking and possessed the charm of sweet talk, but as for substance, all she could see now was how demanding he was, and how often he had been looking out for only himself their entire relationship.

Caleb, on the other hand, was quiet and more guarded so he didn't instantly attract attention. But unlike Bryan, Caleb always put her needs before his own. When he disagreed with her or tried to convince her not to do something, it was because he feared for her—not because he needed to prove himself.

Bryan tightened the hold on her arm and gave her a firm jerk. Unsteady on her feet, Paige tripped forward into him.

"Leave me alone," she said, trying to push his hand off her again. She jerked backwards and her elbow struck the porch railing.

Behind her, the mug of tea hit the ground shattering into jagged pieces.

"Let go of her! What's going on?" Caleb's questions tumbled out loudly as he rounded the corner of the inn's wraparound porch.

The second Paige saw Caleb she relaxed. Bryan couldn't force anything, not with Caleb standing next to her. Not with Caleb protecting her.

"So it was him—the lumberjack from before is the monster who let you get hurt?" Bryan released her arm and sneered at Caleb.

"I don't even know what you're talking about." Paige narrowed her eyes.

Bryan shook his head. "Your mom said you were out on the beach last week and hurt your foot. She said you were rushed to emergency care and not a week later this guy's making you dance on an injury? Real hero type you're palling around with these days. You've known this monster all of a month and he gets you hurt." Almost nose to nose, Bryan stepped into her personal space.

She'd deal with her mother later. "It was a cut." Paige tried to shove Bryan's hand off her arm again.

Wrapping his arm around her, Caleb pulled her to his side—and away from Bryan. "You're the only one here who's hurt Paige."

"Aw. Did I now? Poor Paige. Always playing the victim." Bryan stalked closer again.

Caleb angled his body between them. "You won't lay another hand on her as long as I'm here."

Don't fight. Please don't fight.

With her arm, she slipped her hand into Caleb's and laced her fingers with his. She pumped his hand once, silently asking him to cool down. Caleb didn't know that Bryan was a lawyer. If Caleb threw a punch, Bryan would ruin his life in court on a bunch of trumped-up charges.

Bryan crossed his arms, and a slow, mocking smile played across his face. "I'll never understand you, Paige. You get down on me for seeing other people, but it sure didn't take you long to find a new fan club." He snorted. "Just never figured you to end up with Mr. Farm and Fleet."

Caleb started to talk, but Paige tugged lightly on his arm. This battle was hers to fight. Bryan wanted her to get emotional, too bad for him. His words held no power over her any longer. "You are not welcome here, and you are not welcome in my life."

Bryan fisted his hands and looked back and forth between the two of them. "Forget you. You were always a waste of time, and it won't take long before this new guy realizes that, too, and leaves you for someone better. Let your mom know she owes me forty bucks for gas." He stalked back to his car and kicked it into gear. His tires spun in the gravel as he drove away, forming a new cloud of dust that Paige watched slowly settle back to earth.

Caleb worked his jaw back and forth. It had taken everything in him not to explode at Paige's ex-boyfriend. How could the man talk to her like that? A fraction of his thoughts went to Bryan's words about him—he'd accused Caleb of letting Paige get hurt.

Old guilt gnawed on his conscience.

Stop. Paige's foot was fine. People got hurt sometimes. It was a small cut that had already healed.

Gently, he tugged on her arm and turned her to face

him. "Are you all right?" He searched her eyes for tears but found none.

"I'm fine. Good, actually." A smile played at her lips.

"You sure? Some of that stuff he said…"

"I've never been able to stand up to him like that. I don't think he'll be back."

Caleb smiled back at her. "I don't think so, either. Do you still want to go out?"

"Yeah." She tugged his arm close. "No use letting him ruin our day."

Within ten minutes they were seated at his favorite booth at the Cherry Top Café. He worked the saltshaker around and around in his hand. "There's something I wanted to talk to you about, but I'm not sure right now is a good time anymore."

As she placed a napkin on her lap, Paige quirked an eyebrow.

Caleb rubbed the back of his neck. "I don't want to come off sounding like *him*." He dropped his gaze to the table.

In an instant, her hand covered his. "Look at me."

He obeyed.

"You are nothing like Bryan. Okay? Nothing. I'm just sorry it took me a while to realize that."

The waitress dropped off their food, and Caleb offered a quick prayer before they started eating.

Paige pulled the lettuce off her burger and added more ketchup. "So…I'm all intrigued now. What did you want to talk about?"

He laid down his soup spoon. "It's about Sarah's Home."

"I'm listening."

Caleb shared with her that Timmons asked him to fill in for the basketball coach for the next few weeks. "The game against our school's rival is this Thursday. I can't be in two places at once. I would if I could."

She folded her hands in her lap. "Are you trying to ask me not to go to Sarah's Home this week?"

He nodded, once, slowly.

She looked out the window for a moment. "I know you're asking me not to go only because you care about me, so I won't go."

"Thank you." The hoarse whisper surprised him, but it was all he could manage.

After lunch, they decided to leave Caleb's truck downtown and walked to the dock hand in hand. Local residents and some of their students spotted them and waved or greeted them with smiles and catcalls.

He'd always wondered how the community would react if he started dating again. It seemed as if they were just as excited for him to have a happy ending as he was. Now that Paige understood his need to keep her safe, Caleb allowed himself to picture a long future beside her. Perhaps happy endings could happen more than once in a lifetime—more than that, despite Caleb's mistakes in the past, God was here offering him a second chance at a new beginning.

Chapter Fourteen

The game wouldn't start for another forty minutes, but Paige wanted to catch Caleb and wish him the best before the team took the floor. Arriving so early, she'd be able to snag a seat right behind the team, too.

Her phone vibrated in her hand and she glanced at the screen. It was a text from Tasha, one of the seniors at Sarah's Home.

You coming 2nite? Need help with a scholarship essay. Due tomorrow.

Paige's heart sunk to her toes as she bit her lip. What could she text back? She needed to catch Caleb before the game. Maybe he'd agree that the best thing for her to do would be to go help Tasha. There had to be a compromise. Perhaps she could pick up Tasha and take her somewhere public and safe and they could work on the essay.

Some of the lights were off in the main section of the high school. Game patrons would enter through the gym doors by the ticket counter, but Paige used her school key to stop by her classroom beforehand. Walking in the dark hallways alone brought back every image from every scary movie she'd ever watched.

She picked up her pace. One more turn and she'd be near the back entrance of the gym by the locker rooms. Paige rounded the corner and stopped in her tracks in the dark hallway.

Caleb and Amy stood close together talking near the water fountain outside of the men's locker room. Amy looked like she belonged on a Hollywood red carpet instead of at a small town event in Goose Harbor. In a tight, bloodred dress, she was way overdressed for a basketball game. Paige fought the urge to inch forward and listen in on their conversation. It had to end soon. Amy tapped Caleb's chest and he started to laugh—a genuine, enjoyable laugh. Paige wrapped her fingers over the hair ties lining her wrist.

Caleb opened up his arms and stepped forward, wrapping Amy in a hug.

Before her brain could compute anything, Paige spun on her heels and started back through the dark halls.

Bryan's words from earlier that week whizzed through her mind. *You were always a waste of time, and it won't take long before this new guy realizes that, too, and leaves you for someone better.*

She palmed at the tears that started running down her face and dripping off her chin and jammed the back of her hand into her mouth to bite back a sob.

As much as she didn't want to admit it, Bryan was right. Caleb was no different than the rest of them. He tricked her so easily. Worked his way into her heart just so he could squeeze it dry again. *Stupid Paige.*

Men cheated and lied.

She'd promised herself it wouldn't happen again. And it had. So quickly. What a fool.

Shaking so badly, it took three tries to successfully get her car key in the ignition.

It was less than thirty minutes until the doors opened at Sarah's Home. Tasha needed her—not Caleb.

Paige worked the chain of her necklace around and around in her hand. Going would upset Caleb, but his feelings weren't relevant anymore. The entire reason she came to Goose Harbor had been for a chance to be independent and to follow her heart at Sarah's Home. Getting involved with Caleb had thrown her off course. No more. If she was going to help Tasha, she needed to leave now.

Forty minutes later when she pulled into the parking lot at Sarah's Home, she only counted two cars. Why so few volunteers tonight? She slung her bag over her shoulder, locked her car and went inside.

As for volunteers, only Vick and Marty had showed, and there were only two students.

Her heart sank further into the tips of her gym shoes.

When she'd pictured serving here, she'd imagined a building packed full of students to encourage, inspire and challenge. Face it. Sarah's Home showed signs of clear cardiac arrest.

"Miss Paige, you came!" Tasha called from her spot at a desk in the study room. The girl ran over and gave her a hug. "When I didn't hear back from you I thought you might not show and I was going to tear up what I'd written and just not apply to this scholarship."

"I'm here, and you know what? We're not just going to apply to that scholarship—we're going to win it." Pushing Caleb out of her mind, Paige offered a smile.

Marty peeked his head into the room. "I'm glad you came. Vick's heading out right now so it's just you and me and the couple students. I figure we'll close down early."

Paige set down her bag. Smalls hadn't even showed.

"It's so odd. We usually have ten students or so. How come no one's here tonight?"

Tasha yanked a spiral notebook from her weathered backpack. "They all know Mr. Caleb and some of the others isn't coming tonight. Guess they figured it was near closed."

Vick left, along with the second student. Marty moved into the office to balance the nonprofit's checkbook and go over the mail. Paige and Tasha spent the evening working on her essay. When they were done they called her grandmother to pick her up since there weren't other students for her to walk home with tonight.

After Tasha left, Paige straightened a couple of chairs and washed a few dishes that must not have been taken care of by whoever was in charge of closing up last week.

She ran her hand along the wall on her way to the office to say good-night to Marty. Sarah's Home shouldn't have to shut down just because Caleb couldn't be there on a certain night. They needed more staff, better security measures, and perhaps they could create a partnership between Goose Harbor students and Brookside students. Both needed to see other aspects of the world. They shared proximity but experienced completely different lives. A forged partnership could teach everyone something.

The office door creaked when she entered. The older man had his back to the doorway as he talked on the phone in an animated voice. It sounded like he was saying good-night to his grandchildren, so she decided not to interrupt him.

Outside, another streetlight had burned out, casting the parking lot in shadows. She pulled her keys out of her pocket and clicked for the Mazda to unlock. At the same time she heard a scuffling of feet. Paige whipped around, clutching her purse, her heartbeat pounding in her ears.

No one behind her.

Relax. She breathed a sigh of relief and turned back around.

More footsteps.

She turned to check for someone again, but as she did something very hard bashed into the side of her head. Paige's head lashed sideways. She tried to scream, but it came out more like a moan. Her hands instinctively flew to her throbbing head.

Someone jerked her bag out of her hands.

A series of tiny lights popped in her vision. So dizzy.

As her body tipped forward, she commanded her arms to catch her, but they refused to move. First her knees buckled, and then her chin glanced off the ground. A wave of pain rolled over her as ringing sounded in her ears. Something wet and warm seeped from her chin. She tried to move her head and the warmth found its way to her lips. It tasted metallic. *Blood.*

Footsteps again. Was her attacker still there? Would they shoot her like they did Sarah?

Paige blinked, trying to force her eyes to focus, but everything other than a flash of orange looked blurry.

Her eyelids dared to slip shut but she fought them. She started to shiver. Her teeth chattered even though it wasn't cold.

Voices sounded distant, like people were talking out in the street, but she could feel that they were nearby. Suddenly, as if a veil had been tossed over her brain, everything became hazy.

She let her head slump and everything went black.

The buzzer sounded just as the ball his player lobbed fell with a swoosh into the basket. Caleb high-fived the team when they ran into the locker room for halftime. They gathered on the center bench to hear his pep talk.

His phone vibrated in his back pocket for the tenth time. Safely away from the crowd, he flipped his cell phone open to see who'd been trying to get hold of him all night. He saw Maggie in the crowd during the first half. Did Paige or Shelby need something?

Every missed call came from his buddy Miles, who worked as a police officer in Brookside. Why would Miles call right now? They might have been friends since grade school, but they caught up over a game about once a month—never by phone.

A twenty-pound weight settled to the pit of his gut. *Sarah's Home.*

The use of personal phones wasn't allowed during school functions, but he decided to ignore that rule just this once. Caleb hit the redial button.

Miles answered on the first ring. "I've been trying to get ahold of you for the last hour."

"I saw."

"You need to get down here. Now."

Down here. Brookside?

Caleb lowered his eyebrows and tried to process Miles's words. His friend's voice usually didn't carry such urgency.

He turned his back to the high-school students. "What's going on?"

"That girl you like. The one you've been telling me about. Her name's Paige, right?"

No. Not Paige. Paige was in Goose Harbor. Safe. She'd promised. "Yes."

"She's been hurt. Someone attacked her outside of Sarah's Home and—"

"What happened? Is she…?" Bile rose in his throat and his knees threatened to give way. Hand on his head, he turned in a pointless circle. The basketball team fell silent and all stared at him. He didn't care.

"She's at St. Mike's in the E.R. I'm here, too."

"I'm on my way."

The news hit him like an ice storm. He rocked forward and bounded for the door before Principal Timmons stopped him.

Caleb grabbed the door frame as his world rocked like a Tilt-A-Whirl. "You have to take over as coach. Paige is in the hospital. I have to go."

Timmons's mouth went slack. "Do you know what's wrong?"

Words clogging his throat, Caleb shook his head. Timmons shooed him out of the locker room and promised the team would be fine without him.

Leaving the gym and the rest of the community behind, Caleb hurtled into his truck and stepped on the gas. His heart slammed against his ribs with what felt like enough force to break through bones, and his hands shook as he tried to white-knuckle the wheel.

She'd gone without letting him know after she said she wouldn't. That stung. Their relationship had progressed to more than that in the past few weeks.

Then again, had he known, he would have been crawling up the gym walls during the game with worry. Who was he kidding? He would have stormed out of the game before it started and rushed to Brookside.

Why had she gone tonight when he asked her not to? He warned her something like this would happen.

Something like what? If Paige had been shot…

Don't let the mind go there. She's okay. She has to be.

Caleb drove blindly, ramming his fist against the steering wheel at the red light.

Surrender. He was supposed to be surrendering the care of others to God.

But then something like this happens....

He stopped that train of thought.

Pray. Pray.

But what if? Stop. *Hand it over.*

God. Keep her safe. Protect her. Please don't take her.

His gut corkscrewed. If only he could do something more tangible. Then again, the most impactful tool within his arsenal right now was to pray and hand his worry to God in this moment.

And drive faster.

"Oh, there now. Looks like you're coming to." A woman's voice drifted, like a feather from a busted pillow, until it rested gently on Paige's mind.

A callused hand squeezed hers.

"Paige. Sweetheart. Can you hear me?" The man's voice caused a calming sense to run down her spine like a spring-fed river. *Caleb.*

Paige opened her eyes and discovered she was tucked tightly under the starched white sheets of a hospital bed. Earthy brown covered the walls and a giant painting of a lady on a boat hung on the adjacent wall.

Caleb kissed the back of her hand then cupped it between both of his. "Take it slow, okay…you've been through a lot."

A middle-aged nurse with dyed red hair and a kind smile bent over her. "There you are now. Look at those bright blue eyes."

Paige's head felt crammed full of marshmallows. She blinked deliberately.

Sarah's Home. Footsteps. Her head. That was all she could remember.

And a sharp pain in her chin, which seemed to have subsided some since she fell. Her mind started to race in circles like an animal stuck in a tight cage. She remembered lying on the pavement but couldn't recall coming to the hospital. Had Caleb brought her here? Shouldn't he be back in Goose Harbor? Who put her in this bed?

An image of him wrapping his arms around Amy flooded back into her mind. What happened after she left? Why was he here with her anyway? Nothing made sense.

Confusion started to run around screaming in her head. She wanted to box her ears to block it out and go back to sleep.

Tears pooled in her eyes and threatened to fall. "What happened?"

Caleb scooted his chair as close as he could get to her. She narrowed her eyes to focus on him—really focus. Lines around his eyes, his lips bowing down and a ruffled brow—he looked older tonight. He looked tired and worn down.

"From what we can gather, someone attacked you outside of Sarah's Home." He scrubbed his free hand down his face and rubbed his eyes a couple of times. "You have a good goose egg on the side of your head, and you got a bit of a gash on your chin."

Her hand flew to the numb spot on her chin. *Stitches.* When had they put these in? Why couldn't she remember anything?

Her fingers trembled over each suture. "Give me a mirror."

"It's nothing." He rubbed his thumb on the back of her hand.

"I need a mirror." Shoving off blankets, she started to get up. Caleb's shoulders slumped. The drain of color in his face spoke volumes about her appearance, but she needed to see. He helped her stand and shuffle to the mirror on the wall.

Ugly black thread weaved across her chin. She turned her head right before her vision clouded. "I look like the bride of Frankenstein."

"Come on. Don't say that. You're beau—"

Paige stopped him with a firm hand to his chest. "Don't. Please. Just don't right now." She shoved past him. "I don't even know why you're here."

He tilted his head. "Of course I'm here. I came the second I heard."

A handsome man with a five-o'clock shadow cleared his throat in the doorway. The badge on his uniform glistened under the artificially bright lights in her room. He hooked his hands on his gun belt.

"I'm Officer Reid. You can call me Miles. The doctor says you're going to be okay. Head wounds just bleed a lot. Even the minor ones." The officer's voice was a balm. Strong and reassuring. He was well trained.

Miles stepped farther into the room. "I'd like to ask you a couple questions about what happened tonight."

Any energy she had drained away. Sleep. She wanted sleep.

"I didn't see anything."

He pulled out a note-card-size spiral book from his front shirt pocket. "Unfortunately I still need to get some information so I can start a report and hopefully catch the responsible party."

Caleb stepped in the way, stopping Miles from moving closer. "Can you do this another time? She probably has a concussion and can't think straight right now. We can call you or come to the station once she's feeling up to it if you want, but let's not do this right now."

Miles peeked around Caleb and looked Paige over. Then

he nodded once, sharply, but with the trace of a smile on his lips. "My card." He pulled a business card from his pocket. Then he pointed at Caleb. "Take good care of her."

When the doctor released her to go, Caleb drove his truck up to the front circle and a nurse pushed her out to meet him in a wheelchair. He hopped out, helped her up into the passenger seat and closed the door.

For the first few minutes into the drive home, tension stacked between them like a tangible wall.

Staring out the front window at the black curtain of night, Caleb worked his jaw back and forth. "Paige, I—"

"I don't want to talk to you." Eyes trained out the passenger window, she didn't trust herself to look at him.

"I just wanted to say that I'm glad you're okay." His hand brushed against hers on the bench seat.

She moved her hand into her lap, away from him. Of course he would act like they were still seeing each other. How could he know she'd seen him and Amy together? But she didn't want to talk about it. Not now. This terrible night didn't need to be made worse by enduring a drawn-out relationship conversation.

"Paige," he started again.

"Please. My head is pounding like a rock concert. Just. Don't talk," she whispered and bit her lip.

Don't cry.

Don't cry over another disappointing, cheating man.

Chapter Fifteen

A quick glance in his side mirror said he should have shaved and taken a nap, but Caleb needed to get over to Maggie's and see Paige. She'd acted strange last night. Different and more closed off from him than before.

When he arrived home he'd spent the night combing through paperwork in Sarah's old office, looking for the charter papers for Sarah's Home. She might have left the board in charge, but there had to be a loophole to supersede the board's decisions. And if he couldn't find a way, at the least, he and Paige were done serving there. Maybe it was time to let go of one of his last connections to Sarah in order to keep Paige safe.

After locating the paperwork, the fine print and lawyer talk had given him a good headache, but he'd found the information he'd been looking for. She might have left the board in charge of Sarah's Home, but only Caleb's named appeared on the bank account that paid for the nonprofit. The answer had been in front of him all the time.

So, he might not have the power to declare the nonprofit was done, but he could stop paying the bills. Without the lease, insurance and utilities paid for, the place would have to shut down. So it was settled. As horrible as it made him feel to play the money card, he was closing Sarah's Home. That's all there was to it.

Caleb parked his truck and made his way to the West Oak Inn's blue front steps, where Ida and Maggie sat. "How's our patient?"

Ida reached over to pump his hand once. "Nothing a little love can't fix."

Leave it to Ida, the town romantic, to say something like that.

He fought the smile tugging at his lips. "And how are you two?"

"Beat." Maggie yawned. "This concussion stuff is murder on the sleep cycle."

"How about you both go rest for a while and I'll keep an eye on her?" He helped Ida hobble back to her cottage next door.

"Aren't you supposed to be teaching?" Ida poked him in the ribs.

"Timmons gave me the day off." He made certain Ida was settled in her house before going back to the inn.

He found Paige with a blanket wrapped around her shoulders in Maggie's living room. A scowl on her face announced that she must not be feeling well yet. The stitches on her chin screamed at him—he couldn't keep her safe. Had failed to protect her. Would never be able to take care of her like she needed.

They needed to talk. He had to know why she'd gone to Sarah's Home when he asked her not to.

"I know you're tired, and you've been through a lot, but we really need to talk." He snagged a seat on the armrest near her.

She shifted away from him. "I don't want to talk to you."

Deep breath. "That was fine last night, but not today."

Didn't she realize how much it bothered him that she went to Sarah's Home? She'd promised not to. He deserved to know why she'd gone.

"You don't get to decide that." She crossed her arms.

"Listen." He modulated his voice. "I'm really frustrated with you. I asked one small thing of you and you couldn't—"

Paige exploded to her feet. "You're frustrated with me?" Her voiced reached a level he hadn't heard before. "Well, know what, I'm angry at you. Downright angry. I thought you were someone you're not, and I want nothing to do with you anymore."

He reeled back as if she'd struck him. "What are you talking about?"

She stalked toward him. "I saw you with Amy. Don't act like you weren't with her yesterday."

When had he been with Amy? Only when… "You were at the high school? I never saw you."

"Of course you didn't see me." Her laugh held no humor. "You wouldn't have gotten all cozy with her if you'd known—"

Paige had a history of men cheating on her. Of course her seeing him talking to Amy would have pressed that button. It bothered him that she didn't trust him to be faithful, but hopefully that would come with time.

He raised his hands in a stop motion. "I didn't do anything with her."

"I saw you."

"What? You saw me hug her?" He shrugged. "Yeah, I hugged her. She was there to apologize for how she's acted toward me the last couple years. Seems she had a conversation with you that is making her rethink the way she's been behaving."

Paige stopped pacing "A conversation…with me?"

"Yes."

"I didn't know if she'd taken it to heart or not."

"Evidently she did, because she asked me to forgive her. I'm sorry if offering her a hug hurt you. At the time I thought it was appropriate."

So she watched him interact with Amy and went to Sarah's Home to get at him? He sure hoped not.

Give me patience. I need it.

"So you weren't…?" The fire inside of her defused instantly and she wanted to apologize.

"I would never cheat on someone. Ever." Caleb's voice was low, laced with hurt. "Is that why you went to Sarah's Home?"

"Partially." And because one of the students needed her.

Caleb got to his feet and took her hands. "I get that you were upset, but next time talk to me about it, okay? You can't do things like that when you're not thinking straight. You put yourself in danger and got hurt."

"Right. And that was my choice. Remember, if I get hurt, that's my choice." She tugged on his hands lightly.

He let go of one of them and ran his hand through his hair as he released a stream of air. "But that's the problem. That choice still affects me. Do you understand what you put me through last night? Paige, I was out of my mind when I got the call from Miles. I thought….I thought… My mind went straight there. It was happening all over again."

Her stomach corkscrewed. She really had put him through a lot. Then again, what's to say someone he cared about wouldn't get hurt doing something mundane tomorrow? She could get in a car wreck on the way to the post office. It didn't take going into an urban part of Brookside to be in danger. Why couldn't he understand that?

"I'm sorry you had to relive that. It must have been horrible." She tried to meet his eyes.

"It's okay. We just need to do better at keeping you safe in the future—for both our sakes." His shoulders visibly relaxed. "I found Sarah's paperwork last night and realized there's a way I can shut Sarah's Home down for good."

Paige dropped his hand. "You want to do what?"

"That place was never my dream or passion, and it holds too many bad memories for me now. I just—I want it gone."

"So step down. You can leave." They didn't need him with that sort of attitude anyway. "Don't ruin it for everyone."

"No." He shook his head. "The only way to make the place safe is to close the doors for good."

"Safe for whom? For you? Maybe. But I always thought you cared about more than yourself. Those kids deserve an uplifting place in that town."

He started to pace. "But it's not safe for any of them, and I'm done worrying about what's going to happen there."

"So that means you just need to walk away from it." Paige fisted her hands to keep from shaking. "Leave Sarah's Home to the people who care about it."

"I may have to do that if they open a new account and can raise enough money to keep the doors open. If they do, then I still want you and me to stop working there. We're done."

She rounded toward him, almost coming nose to nose. "You can't tell me what to do. Even though I know you think you're doing the right thing to keep me safe, all you're really doing is keeping yourself safe. Don't you see that? In the end, it still feels an awful lot like control."

"This is important to me, Paige." He rested his hands on her shoulders. "If you want to be with me, I don't want you at Sarah's Home. It's that simple. I've worried even when I've been there and been able to protect you. But now what I've feared happening has come true, so I was right about the danger. Let's just be done."

"Let me get this straight—it's stay at Sarah's Home and lose you, or stay with you and never go back to Sarah's Home?"

He nodded.

She shrugged out of his hold. "That's ridiculous."

"It's fair. And it's only if I can't close Sarah's Home, which I'm pretty certain that I can."

"I was so wrong about you." She stepped away from him and turned her back. "You know, I somehow fooled myself into thinking you were this caring guy, but you're not. You're just as controlling as Bryan was."

"Don't compare me to him." He raised his voice slightly.

"I guess I don't want to be with you, then. I choose Sarah's Home." She grabbed the door handle and flung open the door. "You can leave."

Caleb walked through the doorway, but when he reached the porch he turned back to face her. "Are you sure that's what you want?"

"Positive. And if you try to close it, you better be ready for my fight. My dad's a lawyer after all, and his counsel's only a call away." She quickly turned and shut the door.

At least with the door closed she couldn't see the hurt look in his eyes anymore. The one that made her want to cry uncle and tell him she wanted to be with him and they could work this out.

A moment later, she leaned against the thick door and slid down to the ground. It was better this way. Better without Caleb in her life. Better alone.

Right?

* * *

Saturday morning, Caleb sat at the kitchen table letting his cereal get soggy.

His normal routine would include stopping by the farmer's market with Shelby and then heading over to Maggie's to see if she needed anything, or if he could catch Paige.

Not today.

"Are you sure you won't come with me?" Shelby bumped her elbow to his.

He scrubbed his hand over the stubble on his chin. Maybe he should shave. No, he'd wait until Sunday night. "I need some time to myself. You know how I am."

"You aren't going to eat this, are you?" She grabbed his bowl and dumped it into the sink. Shelby kept her back to him for a moment, and then she whirled around, her eyes bright. "Know what? I do know you, and sometimes you need to be alone, but other times you need to hear it like it is. Most of the time, you don't get that second part because everyone's afraid to say anything challenging to you."

"Oh, really?" Caleb leaned back in his chair. This ought to be interesting.

Always a stream of constant movement, Shelby straightened a pile of mail while she talked. "You've got to stop blaming yourself for everything that happens to people. You assume too much responsibility."

Caleb splayed his hands out on the table and stared at his work-worn fingers.

Next she conquered the trash can, yanking out the bag as she spoke and putting in a new lining without skipping a word. "Here's the thing. You can't change what happens to people, but you can change your response."

Great. Something else he'd been doing wrong. Not trusting God, assuming and something about how he responded to things. Pile it on.

"For example." She grabbed the dishrag and washed down the counter. "When I got hurt you said it was your fault."

Resting his elbows on his knees, Caleb put his head in his hands. Why would she bring that up? "Because it *was* my fault. I pushed you out when you wanted to talk that day. If I hadn't you wouldn't—"

She clunked plates together loudly, making it impossible to speak for a moment.

He raised his eyebrows to her, trying to convey a brotherly knock-that-off cue.

Jutting the dish towel in his direction, she let out a huff. "Unless you have a time machine you're not telling me about, you have absolutely no clue what could have happened had something gone differently. We can't change the past, but you do get a chance to shape the present. But, bro, you've been living in the past a long time—and not just since Sarah. This problem started years before that."

Shelby dropped the rag into the sink then crossed back to her vacated chair. She laid her hand on top of his, and her voice grew quiet. "It was my choice—not yours—to go to the church the night we found out Dad was leaving. Just like it was Sarah's choice that night to go to Brookside and Paige's choice the other night."

Then why did he feel like he'd failed them?

Emotions clogged his speech and burned the back of his eyes.

He cleared his throat. "Tell me what's so bad about not wanting people to get hurt."

"Nothing…except that the pain-free life you want everyone to have would be one without growth." She squeezed his hand.

"So you're saying it's a good thing that you got burned? Because that's ludicrous, Shelby." He pulled his hand gently away so hers thudded on the table. "You should have never had to endure that."

She pulled her sleeves so they rode low on her wrists. "But I did. So instead of saying it shouldn't have happened, you need to accept that it happened and decide what that means and how that circumstance will shape you moving forward. I did. But you don't do that. You stay rooted in the past and focus on what could have been."

Caleb braced his elbows on the table and stared at her. "You've been wanting to say that for a long time, haven't you?"

Rising from the table, Shelby smoothed out her hair in the hallway mirror and grabbed her canvas bag for the market. "Today seemed like the right time."

With her hand on the knob, she looked at him over her shoulder. "Good talk?"

"I guess."

Flashing a smile, she left out the front door. Caleb cradled his forehead in his hand. So much to consider. Why hadn't he processed through these issues before now? Because no one thought to confront him.

The front door swung back open. "Oh, and Caleb, go win Paige back."

Right. Paige. Her ability to stand up to him had been the catalyst to so much introspection lately. Good stuff. Things like what Shelby just said.

But Paige didn't want to be with him. At least, not romantically. She'd made that clear yesterday.

"I don't know if she'll want to see me again. I made a lot of stupid mistakes."

"Remember." She knocked on her head. "Don't dwell on past circumstances—learn from them. And side note, Paige will want to see you again. I'm sure of that." Shelby blew him a kiss and walked out the door.

Perhaps Shelby was right.

The door swung open again. "Oh, and if you do have a time machine—I want in on that."

"Go to the market." He grabbed a nearby throw pillow and pretended to lob it at her.

She giggled and finally left.

Or maybe Shelby was crazy.

Chapter Sixteen

She should be paying attention to the minister speaking up front, but Paige kept craning her neck to locate Caleb in the small crowd in the church. Since the service took place in a movie theater, it was hard to see people who sat in the last few high rows. Was he up there? If so, they needed to talk before they saw each other at school tomorrow and things became awkward. Moreover, Paige had to get him to agree to a compromise to keep Sarah's Home open.

After the closing song, Paige flagged down Shelby. "Where's your brother?"

Shelby grabbed both her hands and pumped them. "Oh, you know. Off being moody in nature somewhere. Please don't give up on him."

"If you see him will you tell him I want to talk?"

"I'll do better. I'll tie him up, toss him in my trunk and drive him over to Maggie's." Shelby opened her arms for a hug. She pulled Paige close and whispered, "He loves you, even if he's never told you that."

Heart fluttering like a caged hummingbird, Paige slipped on her sunglasses and walked outside. Caleb loved her? He couldn't...so soon. Right?

After church Maggie drove Paige into Brookside to pick

up her car. Paige would have picked it up sooner, but she'd had so much on her mind and Marty had promised to check on it every day. Besides, she refused to live in fear that something would happen to her car or to her every time she ventured out of the safe bubble of Goose Harbor.

"Are you sure you're good to drive?" Maggie asked for the seventh time as they pulled into the parking lot of Sarah's Home.

"Promise." Paige took her purse. "Don't wait for me. There's something I have to do in town. I should be home by dinner."

Maggie rolled down her window and yelled, "Do you have a cell on you?"

"Mine was on the floor of my car when I drove here, and I brought a charger in my purse." She fished the cord out and waved it for Maggie to see. "I'll be fine."

It felt weird to drive again after three days of not being allowed. Pulling out the folded directions she'd printed off from the city website, Paige turned onto Ashland Square and saw the police station right away. No one knew, but she had called Miles before church and set up an appointment to come speak with him about the attack.

Miles greeted her with a smile and an offer of coffee. He steered her into a small interview room off the lobby. "How have you been feeling?"

Paige gave him a warm smile. "I'm fine. I'm sorry it took me a couple days to make it out here, but I'm ready to talk about what happened—and who I think the offender might be." Orange shoes running away. She shook her head to shoo away the image. "But I have a concern because I don't want them to get in trouble—especially if the person is a juvenile."

Eyes narrowed in a thoughtful way, Miles tilted his head. "We have a couple options if it's a juvenile. However, since an assault took place there will have to be a consequence of some sort. Now—I have to ask, do you know who attacked you?"

Fiddling with the strap on her purse she considered not telling, but that would be lying. "Do you know Smalls Avaro?"

"Albert? Yeah, his brothers are both regulars."

"I think he did it."

"One of his brothers?"

"No, Smalls. I mean Albert. And I actually think I know where we can find him."

Caleb tossed a stone into the lake. All the teens he taught could get them to skip, but he'd never figured out how to flick his wrist correctly.

He turned a well-worn rock over and over in his hand.

As much as he didn't want to admit it, Shelby and Paige were both right. In the past few hours he'd assessed what his life after Sarah's death consisted of.

Basically, it had become pathetic.

Not counting his job, besides his jogs and reading and the occasional pick-up game of basketball with the students, he had no life outside of taking care of others. Which wouldn't be terrible, but his motives hadn't always been pure. He hadn't taken charge in a manner to serve them. Instead, he made them dependent on him so he felt important. Like he had worth.

He'd chided Paige for not realizing her worth and searching for it in the wrong place, but really, he was no different.

Slipping the stone into his pocket, he shuffled his feet in the sand.

Paige pointed out once that the whole town enabled him in his vain desire to protect everyone and overcontrol situations. She'd been right. After Sarah, they'd all gone out of their way to make him feel useful and needed. Problem being, he'd moved from caring about people to trying to handle everything in their lives so he could keep them from getting hurt. Which, like Shelby pointed out, sometimes kept them from growing.

Fact was, if he was in charge of protecting people, he'd always fail.

Caleb dropped to the ground and brought his legs close to his chest so he could lay his forehead on his knees. The wind picked up down the beach, creating a whistling sound in the grass. Seagulls squawked a couple of yards away.

He bowed his head to pray. *You care more about the people I love than I do, don't You? Forgive me for not trusting that before. I do now.*

What would he do now, though?

Love them. His job was to love those people in all their circumstances and to show them grace. The students at Sarah's Home marched through his mind. He'd been a poor example to them and almost considered shutting down their safe haven in town. No more. They deserved his respect just as much as his students in Goose Harbor.

Sarah's Home wouldn't be closing.

Paige scanned the parking lot at the high school. No cars.

She'd stopped by Caleb's house, but his sister said he hadn't been home yet. School tomorrow could be awkward if they didn't talk tonight. They had to make peace about Sarah's Home and their broken relationship, if only to make working together manageable. Then again, perhaps they weren't meant to.

Go home, Paige.

Tracing her normal walking route to and from school,

she turned onto the street that led to Maggie's inn. Color in her peripheral vision made her slam on her brakes. Ida's flowers.

She turned on her hazard lights, put her car in Park and stepped onto the bridge. Sweet Ida with her constant reminders to keep her heart open to love.

Why hadn't she listened?

Since her first day in Goose Harbor, Caleb had been there for her. It burned to know she'd entertained the thought of him cheating on her. If any man was loyal, it was the one who devoted himself to his late wife's dream.

Caleb proved to be everything she never thought any man could be. He cared about his family, watched out for people in need, took his faith seriously and treated her with dignity.

Yes, he tried to control things more than he should, but the source came from love. He wanted to shelter the people he cared about. Was that so bad?

"And I love him." The words came so suddenly she slapped a hand over her mouth. But they were true.

Running her fingers on the soft flower petals, she leaned in, breathing their bee-luring perfume.

"I botched everything," she whispered. "Didn't I?"

Not wanting to go straight back home after such a revelation, Paige climbed back in her car and turned it in the direction of the dunes nature park. She hadn't returned there since cutting her foot, but it struck her as the ideal place to figure out what to say to Caleb and pray.

It only took ten minutes to get there and park, and another fifteen to hike out to the beach area on the dunes. A downed tree made for a perfect bench, and after a cursory look, she slipped off her shoes and sank her feet into the cool layer of sand.

Closing her eyes, she tipped her head back to let the

sun's warmth wash over her face. A moment later, a cloud must have passed in front of the sun because it got darker. Except that didn't make sense, seeing as the sky had been cloudless when she walked down there. Still dark. She opened her eyes.

"Caleb." She breathed his name and the rest of her voice caught in her throat.

He looked down at the ground. Shuffled his feet. "Can we talk? Or if you want to be left alone, that's okay, too. I understand."

"You're here." She was having a hard time being eloquent. The man standing a few feet away was the love she'd dreamed about her whole life. Overcome by the thought, she sprang to her feet and reached for him.

Caleb shook his head and stepped forward where his gentle hands found a home on her shoulders. "I can't stop thinking about you. I'm so afraid I messed up what we had."

Paige lifted one of his hands from her shoulder and leaned her cheek into his open palm. Savoring the feel of his calloused fingers against her soft skin, she closed her eyes. "The last time we talked I was so cruel to you. I'm sorry. I shouldn't have said any of those things."

"I said a lot of terrible things, too. We both have a lot of hurt to bring to the table, but I think it's worth getting through it all to be together." His thumb traced back and forth in the hair above her ear. "I'm not going to close Sarah's Home."

"Really?"

"A lot of the security needs to change before I'm comfortable with it staying open, but that is the only safe place for so many students in Brookside. It stays open, and you're welcome there whenever the door is unlocked. I'm sorry I tried so hard to overprotect you."

She nodded a bunch of times and swallowed hard. "You know, someone caring enough to want to protect me isn't so bad after all."

He framed her face. "I'm not good at this stuff—being in a relationship. Sarah and I were kids when we decided we'd get married. So I missed learning all the dating rules in high school. But if you'll…" He stopped for a moment and leaned so they could have eye contact. "I know it sounds silly, but would you be my girlfriend?"

Paige gave a rapid-nod answer. "Yes."

"Really?" He squeezed her shoulder. "I might make a couple more mistakes along the way. Actually, I can promise you I'll make a lot of mistakes."

"I love you." The words were out before she'd considered saying them, but they were true.

"I love you, too."

A small smile pulled at his lips, and when he opened his arms she didn't waste a minute flying into them. Pressing her face into his neck, she breathed in his familiar pine-and-midnight smell. It felt like home.

His fingers found the soft skin at the nape of her neck. Tipping her head back, Caleb kissed her deeply, and Paige returned the kiss with equal fervor, drinking in the man she thought she'd lost.

When they parted, he pressed his forehead to hers for a minute with his eyes still closed. "This is all too good to be true."

"Walk with me." She unwound from his arms and reached to lace her fingers with his. "We have so much to talk about."

"Only if you do one thing first." Caleb winked. "Put your shoes on."

Tugging her gym shoes back on, she laughed. Only Caleb would remember about her foot getting cut after sharing such a great kiss, but she no longer minded taking small precautions if they made Caleb feel better.

They moved up the beach as the tide rolled in higher. A flock of seagulls scuttled away as they walked nearer.

Paige took a deep breath. "I went to Brookside today."

"Oh?" Caleb's tone held none of the censure she'd feared.

"I met with Miles and we found the person who attacked me."

His grip tightened.

She pumped his hand once. "It was Smalls."

He stopped, causing her to jerk backward by a foot. "Smalls? But he likes you. That makes no sense."

"It didn't for me, either, until we talked to him. His brother's gang tried to recruit him. They had a gun to his head and instructed him to do it or face punishment." She faced Caleb. "He doesn't want to end up in a gang. Smalls has dreams—he wants to go to college and get a degree to help him become a writer. Isn't that great?"

Brow scrunched, Caleb scanned the horizon. "Miles will have to arrest him. That'll ruin his chances of going to school."

"Your friend Miles is great. He made arrangements for Smalls to serve as an informant so the police department can capture some of the major gang members in town in exchange for his charges being dropped. They fingerprinted him, but as long as he doesn't have any more trouble in Brookside for the year, the charges will never be filed. Miles promised to keep an eye on Smalls and have him protected if any of the gangs start to suspect him."

Using one finger, Caleb tucked her wind-blown hair behind her ear. "You're amazing. Most people would have wanted him punished."

"I want him to have a future. That's the kind of impact a place like Sarah's Home can have on a community."

"I agree." He tugged her hand so they could keep walking toward the magenta sun as it began to dip into the onyx horizon. "But we need to raise money for security cameras and a fenced parking lot. Small things like that to make the place safer for everyone."

"I have ideas for changes, too." Paige swung their hands as they walked.

"I can't wait to hear them." He stopped then, and pulled Paige in front of him so her back was against his chest. Wrapping his arms around her, he rested his chin on her head. They stood there until the sun finally dipped below the edge of the lake. "We should head home."

Paige laced her fingers with his and realized Caleb was wrong about one thing. All of this wasn't too good to believe.

Hadn't God directed them on this path all along? Even through the difficult circumstances in life they had both faced before meeting each other. God had taken two broken and hurt people and made them new.

More than that, He now offered them a new start— together.

* * * * *

Dear Reader,

Know what always amazes me about God? No matter what I have done or how I have failed, He'll offer me as many new starts as I ask for. Isn't that comforting? Our God believes in second chances.

Both Paige and Caleb needed fresh starts, but their hesitation to begin again is understandable. As the story starts, Caleb is wrapped in guilt over the death of his late wife. He believes he doesn't deserve a chance to love and live again. On the other hand, Paige is terrified of getting hurt. She has good reason to feel that way. She's been let down by a lot of people she should have been able to count on.

Have you ever felt stuck by your circumstances, by past pain or something you've done? I have good news— God's waiting to offer you a do-over. All that's left is to ask Him for it.

Thank you for spending some time with Paige and Caleb. I hope you enjoyed their story and come back to visit Goose Harbor again. I love interacting with readers on Facebook, Twitter and at my website, www.jessicakellerbooks.com. Look me up and make sure to say hi!

Dream Big,
Jess

Questions for Discussion

1. Paige has a lot of reasons to distrust men. Did you find Paige's transformation to be believable, or not? How come?

2. Because of multiple betrayals in her past, Paige pushes Caleb away from the first time she meets him. Do you think this was appropriate for her to do? What other boundaries could someone set up, and what other ways could someone in Paige's situation guard her heart?

3. A lot of Paige's healing came through her friendships with Maggie, Ida, Bree and Shelby. It's important to have people in your life that can give advice, listen to you and challenge you. For those that don't have a support system like this, what are some ways we can go about forming one? How important is it to you to have someone to bounce ideas off and process with?

4. Can you identify with Paige's lack of desire to read her Bible at the beginning of the story? Caleb suggested she picture the Bible as a new love letter waiting to be read every day. Does thinking of the Bible in this way change the way you think about it? Can you think of one time when you felt God was speaking to you through a Bible story?

5. People that Caleb loves have been hurt and killed. Do you find his need to protect people understandable or a little overboard? If you could sit down with Caleb, what verses and advice would you share with him?

6. Sarah's Home is a nonprofit organization in the midst of a rough city, and the danger the volunteers face is very real. Is it worth the risk to have people staff an outreach like this? What are some ways they could have made Sarah's Home safer from the beginning? Paige feels strongly about Sarah's Home and believes the risk is worth the benefit. What is something you are passionate about that might be scary or risky? Have you pursued that passion, or decided not to?

7. For a long time, Paige didn't feel like she was allowed to stand up for herself. In the two instances where she had to deal with Bryan, do you think she handled herself correctly? If so, what do you believe she did correctly? If not, what could she have done differently?

8. Sometimes we get stuck at a point in our life because of something that happens to us. For Caleb, he felt stuck by guilt, whereas Paige was trapped by things other people had done to her. When we find ourselves stuck like Caleb and Paige did, what are some positive ways that we can move forward in our lives? Can you think of some stories in the Bible where someone was stuck like this? How did God treat them? How did they get unstuck?

9. Paige is warned multiple times to stay away from Amy, but she seeks Amy out after hearing the students making fun of her. Amy doesn't react warmly, and it doesn't look like the two will ever share a close friendship. Can you think of a time when you reached out to someone and it wasn't received well? Was it worth it? If given the chance, would you do it again?

10. When Paige sees Caleb hug Amy she immediately jumps to the conclusion that he must be cheating on her. Can you remember a time when you read a situation incorrectly? What happened as a result of that?

11. When Paige wakes up from the attack, she knows who hurt her but doesn't tell Officer Miles right away. How do you feel about her not sharing about Smalls until later? Should Smalls have faced a stiffer punishment, or was it appropriate to offer him grace? What were some of Paige's other options? If you were in a situation like this, what would you want to happen to Smalls?

12. Caleb asked Paige not to go to Sarah's Home when he has to be at the basketball game. How does it make you feel that he asked that of her? Does he have that right? In what situation and relationship is someone allowed to ask things like that? Are they ever? Should Paige feel badly about going? Why or why not?

13. If you could write an epilogue, what would it say? What hurdles, if any, do you see in Caleb and Paige's future? What advice would you give them as they work to strengthen their relationship?

REQUEST YOUR FREE BOOKS!

2 FREE INSPIRATIONAL NOVELS
PLUS 2
FREE
MYSTERY GIFTS

YES! Please send me 2 FREE Love Inspired® novels and my 2 FREE mystery gifts (gifts are worth about $10). After receiving them, if I don't wish to receive any more books, I can return the shipping statement marked "cancel." If I don't cancel, I will receive 6 brand-new novels every month and be billed just $4.74 per book in the U.S. or $5.24 per book in Canada. That's a saving of at least 21% off the cover price. It's quite a bargain! Shipping and handling is just 50¢ per book in the U.S. and 75¢ per book in Canada.* I understand that accepting the 2 free books and gifts places me under no obligation to buy anything. I can always return a shipment and cancel at any time. Even if I never buy another book, the two free books and gifts are mine to keep forever.

105/305 IDN F47Y

Name	(PLEASE PRINT)	
Address		Apt. #
City	State/Prov.	Zip/Postal Code

Signature (if under 18, a parent or guardian must sign)

Mail to the Harlequin® Reader Service:
IN U.S.A.: P.O. Box 1867, Buffalo, NY 14240-1867
IN CANADA: P.O. Box 609, Fort Erie, Ontario L2A 5X3

**Are you a subscriber to Love Inspired books
and want to receive the larger-print edition?
Call 1-800-873-8635 or visit www.ReaderService.com.**

* Terms and prices subject to change without notice. Prices do not include applicable taxes. Sales tax applicable in N.Y. Canadian residents will be charged applicable taxes. Offer not valid in Quebec. This offer is limited to one order per household. Not valid for current subscribers to Love Inspired books. All orders subject to credit approval. Credit or debit balances in a customer's account(s) may be offset by any other outstanding balance owed by or to the customer. Please allow 4 to 6 weeks for delivery. Offer available while quantities last.

Your Privacy—The Harlequin® Reader Service is committed to protecting your privacy. Our Privacy Policy is available online at www.ReaderService.com or upon request from the Harlequin Reader Service.

We make a portion of our mailing list available to reputable third parties that offer products we believe may interest you. If you prefer that we not exchange your name with third parties, or if you wish to clarify or modify your communication preferences, please visit us at www.ReaderService.com/consumerschoice or write to us at Harlequin Reader Service Preference Service, P.O. Box 9062, Buffalo, NY 14269. Include your complete name and address.

LI13R

"They're so cute," Brody said.

"Who can't like kittens?" Hannah scooped up another one and held it close, rubbing her nose over the tiny head.

"I meant your kids are cute."

Hannah looked up at him, the kitten still cuddled against her face, appearing surprisingly childlike. Her features were relaxed and she didn't seem as tense as when he'd met her the first time. Her smile dived into his heart. "Well, you're talking to the wrong person about them. I think my kids are adorable, even when they've got chocolate pudding smeared all over their mouths."

He felt a gentle contentment easing into his soul and he wanted to touch her again. To connect with her.

Chrissy patted the kitten and then pushed it away, lurching to her feet.

"Chrissy. Gentle," Hannah admonished her.

"The kitten is fine," Brody said, rescuing the kitten as Chrissy tottered a moment, trying to get her balance on the bunched-up blanket. "Here you go," he said to the mother cat, laying her baby beside her.

Hannah also put her kitten back. She took a moment to stroke Loco's head as if assuring her, then picked up her son and swung him into her arms. "Thanks for taking Corey out on the horse. I know I sounded…irrational, but my reaction was the result of a combination of factors. Ever since the twins were born, I've felt overly protective of them."

"I'm guessing much of that has to do with David's death."

"Partly. Losing David made me realize how fragile life is and, like I told your mother, it also made me feel more vulnerable."

"I wouldn't have done anything to hurt Corey." Brody felt he needed to assure her of that. "You can trust me."

Hannah looked over at him and then gave him a careful smile. "I know that."

Her quiet affirmation created an answering warmth and a faint hope.

Once again he held her gaze. Once again he wanted to touch her. To make a connection beyond the eye contact they seemed to be indulging in over the past few days.

Will Hannah Douglas find love again with handsome rancher and firefighter Brody Harcourt?
Find out in
HER MONTANA TWINS
by Carolyne Aarsen,
available September 2014 from Love Inspired® Books.

LIEXP0814

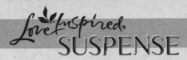
Biologist Dr. Tessa Cleary shielded her eyes against the late summer sun. She surveyed her surroundings and filled her lungs with the sweet scent of fresh mountain air. Tall conifers dominated the forest, but she detected many deciduous trees as well, which surrounded the sparkling shores of the reservoir lake.

A hidden paradise. One to be enjoyed by those willing to venture to the middle of the Pacific Northwest.

The lake should be filled with boats and swimmers, laughing children, fishing poles and water skis.

But all was still.

Silent.

The seemingly benign water filled with something toxic harming both the wildlife and humans.

Her office had received a distressing call yesterday that dead trout had washed ashore and recreational swimmers were presenting with respiratory distress after swimming in the lake.

As a field biologist for the U.S. Forestry Service Fish and Aquatics Unit, her job was to determine what exactly that "something" was as quickly as possible and stop it.

"Here she is!" a booming voice full of anticipation rang out.

A mixed group of civilians and uniformed personnel gathered on the wide, wooden porch of the ranger station.

All eyes were trained on her. All except one man's.

Tall, with dark hair, he stood in profile talking to the sheriff. Too many people blocked him from full view for her to see an agency logo on his forest-green uniform.

Tessa turned her attention to Ranger Harris. "Do you have any idea where the contamination is originating?"

He shook his head. "We haven't come across the source. At least not on our side of the lake. I'm not sure what's happening across the border." George ran a hand through his graying hair as his gaze strayed to the lake. "Whatever this is, it isn't coming from our side."

"Let's not go casting aspersions on our friends to the north until we know more. Okay, George?"

The deep baritone voice came from Tessa's right. She turned to find herself confronted by a set of midnight-blue eyes. Curiosity lurked in the deep depths of the attractive man towering over her.

Answering curiosity rose within her. Who was he? And why was he here?

For more, pick up DANGER AT THE BORDER.
Available September 2014
wherever Love Inspired books are sold.

Love Inspired®

Her Hometown Hero

by

Margaret Daley

In a split second, a tragic accident ends Kathleen Somers's ballet career. Her dreams shattered, she returns home to the Soaring S ranch…and her first love. Suddenly the local veterinarian, Dr. Nate Sterling, goes from her ex to her champion. With the help of a lively poodle therapy dog, the cowboy vet sets out to challenge Kathleen's strength and heal her heart. He'll show her there's life beyond dance, even if it means she leaves town again. But maybe, just maybe, he'll convince her there's only one thing in life worth having… and he's standing right in front of her.

Loving and loyal, these dogs mend hearts.

Available September 2014
wherever Love Inspired books and ebooks are sold.

Find us on Facebook at
www.Facebook.com/LoveInspiredBooks

LI87908